Praise for Christopher Andrews' novels

PANDORA'S GAME

"Christopher Andrews is an exceptional writer and a master of storytelling ... his characters have complex and often unexpected traits that give them a strong emotional resonance ... completely engrossing ... Rarely does a book come along that is so well written that I can't tolerate interruption. A book that's so well written that I can't tolerate it interrupting *itself* is unheard of. To maintain this level of complexity for twenty-one chapters is an incredible storytelling feat."

— Marcus Alexander Hart
Author of *The Oblivion Society*

"Andrews shows versatility ... as much competence and style as Poppy Z. Brite or Anne Rice ... BOOK OF THE MONTH."

— Lesley Meade, *Booknet*

"... incredible ... sharp ... creative ... original and interesting ideas driving the plot and drama ... an ending like a kick in the gut."

— Alex Zawacki, *Class-B*

OF WOLF AND MAN
IPPY AWARD-WINNING BRONZE MEDALIST IN HORROR

"Outstanding sequel! ... everything that a sequel should be ... interesting and creepy ... addresses some bold issues, and does so very well."

— John Howard, *Book Reader 222*

D0939541

DREAM PARLOR

"... the wunderkind Christopher Andrews... one of my top favorite authors ... delighted me again ... a great book ... extremely well-written prose."

— Grabbermcgrew, *Sharp Writer Reviews*

"[Impressive] characters ... An amazing read ... [will] appeal to a much wider audience than the usual science fiction crowd."

— Lesley Meade, *Booknet*

"Excellent from beginning to end ... Andrews has a way with words ... This book is captivating!"

— Julianna Smith
Author of the *Dream Catcher* series

PARANORMALS

"... another delightful journey ... writing style is intriguing ... has the ability to draw the reader [in] ... highly recommended ..."

— Diane Sewell, Denisemclark.com

"EXCELLENT ... elevates [superhumans to a] meaningful level ... more depth than you might expect ... interesting [style] ... impressive skill ... loved this book ..."

— John Howard, *Book Reader 222*

"Andrews is a master of character development ... [we] see their motivations and dreams ... richly executed personalities [drive] the plot forward ..."

— Marcus Alexander Hart
Author of *Caster's Blog*

NIGHT OF THE
LIVING DEAD

Other Works by Christopher Andrews

NOVELS

Pandora's Game
Dream Parlor
Paranormals
Hamlet: Prince of Denmark
Of Wolf and Man
(Bronze IPPY winner for Horror)

COLLECTIONS

The Darkness Within

SCREENPLAYS

Thirst
Dream Parlor
(written with Jonathan Lawrence)
Mistake
One More Round
(a.k.a. *Fighter*, written with Roberto Estrella)

WEB SERIES

Duet

VIDEO GAMES

Bankjob

NIGHT OF THE
LIVING DEAD

A Novelization by
CHRISTOPHER ANDREWS

Adapted from the public domain film
Night of the Living Dead
by
JOHN RUSSO and GEORGE ROMERO

Rising Star Visionary Press trade paperback edition: October, 2009

A Rising Star Visionary Press book
for extra copies please contact by e-mail at
risingstarvisionarypress@earthlink.net
or send by regular mail to
Rising Star Visionary Press
Copies Department
P O Box 9226
Fountain Valley, CA 92728-9226

With absolute respect for the film's creators,
John Russo and *George Romero*.

And thank you to *Daniel* and *Lindsey* at
Rising Star Visionary Press for this opportunity.

BARBRA

"They're coming to get you, Barbra ..."

Barbra jerked, her head snapping upright with painful rigidity. Her neck burned in protest, and she bit down on a gasp the barest instant before it escaped her lips. If Johnny realized that she had fallen asleep while he had to drive ...

But a glance from the corner of her eye showed that her brother had not noticed. He was grumbling under his breath again, too wrapped up in his own bad mood to pay attention to her, for now.

Barbra breathed a sigh of relief, her heart slowing to a more normal pace — not that she would be able to release all of her tension until they got this over with. She glanced out the open passenger-side window, using her blonde hair as a curtain as she looked out at the pretty yet mundane scenery.

What was it that had startled her? A dream that was just beginning to unfold ...

No, not a dream. Not really. A *memory*. A memory of the place they were going, a place she dreaded so much, of her brother chasing her around like a cruel idiot, terrifying his baby sister with his hackneyed Boris Karloff impression. Under other circumstances, she might have mentioned it, using a feint of shared humor to ease her nerves, to try and force her adulthood to scoff her inner child into submission.

But no, it would not be a good idea to remind Johnny of his juvenile games. Lord knew Johnny could be a handful at the best of times, and today's annual errand had already put him into a foul mood.

Johnny had been difficult all day. But then, Johnny was *always* difficult.

Life had not been especially kind to either of them. Their father had died when they were both very young. In spite of their mother's shaky health, she had been forced to take a job as a seamstress, leaving them to spend their days with a grandfather who was not known for his warmth. He had been a church-going man — "church-going" as in the Hellfire & Brimstone variety. His long lectures and sermons had influenced Barbra to attend church to this day (though she preferred a *quieter* church to the one her grandfather had insisted they attend as children), but they had driven Johnny to grow up boisterous and irreverent. This attitude led to frequent conflicts with their grandfather, their mother, and even Barbra on any number of occasions.

Such as today.

Barbra was doing everything she could to keep things civil. She knew that Johnny hated these long trips out to their father's grave, but Johnny owned a car and she didn't, so she had been trying to keep the peace. When the car radio had stopped working about an hour ago, leading to a litany of curse words from Johnny, Barbra had bitten her tongue to avoid voicing her disapproval, which would have only created more tension. He was also chain-smoking cigarette after cigarette, something he *knew* she hated ... but she said nothing.

At long last, they turned onto the winding dirt and gravel road that slithered its lazy way up to the cemetery. Their ritual for the sad anniversary of their father's death was halfway over.

Johnny had ceased his quiet grumbling, and when he

pulled the car into their usual spot near the top of the hill, Barbra offered a light comment. "They ought to make the day the time changes the first day of summer."

Johnny was in the middle of crushing out his cigarette. "What?"

"Well," she explained, "it's eight o'clock and it's still light."

"A lot of good the extra daylight does us," Johnny groused as he futzed with his silly leather driving gloves. "Now we've still got a three-hour drive back. We're not going to be home until after midnight."

"Well if it *really* bugged you, Johnny," she observed, "you wouldn't do it."

She realized as soon as the words left her mouth that it was a mistake, but fortunately, Johnny did not rise to the bait with his usual vehemence. He just snorted and said, "You think I *wanna* blow Sunday on a scene like *this*? You know, I figure we're either gonna have to move Mother out here or move the grave into Pittsburgh."

Barbra rankled and reminded him, "She can't make a trip like this."

"Ohhh," Johnny scoffed as he twisted around to reach into the backseat. "It's not that she can't ... Is there any of that candy left?"

Barbra leaned forward to look. "No."

Johnny pulled the small wreath onto his lap. "Look at this thing," he grumbled. " 'We still remember.' *I* don't. You know, I don't even remember what the man *looks* like."

The sad thing was, she couldn't tell if he really meant it or was just trying to provoke a reaction from her. "Johnny," she sighed, "it takes you five minutes ..."

"Yeah, 'five minutes' to put the wreath on the grave, and *six hours* to drive back and forth. Mother wants to remember, so *we* trot two hundred miles into the country and *she* stays at home."

Weary and wanting to close the subject, Barbra rolled up her window and returned to her placating voice. "Well, we're here, John, all right?"

Johnny mumbled some retort, but he, too, began rolling up his window. Barbra got out of the car and crossed around behind it, her heels crunching on the gravel and making her feel a bit unbalanced. Very faintly, she heard the radio start to whistle through Johnny's rising window.

Now *it decides to work!* she thought.

As she waited for Johnny to catch up, she was only vaguely aware of the voice on the radio saying something about technical problems. She was too busy looking around the graveyard in the dimming light, and struggling to keep her jittery nerves from getting the best of her.

They're coming to get you, Barbra ...

Barbra shuddered. She had never liked graveyards. Pulling her coat tighter around her throat, she stepped off the road and onto the cemetery lawn just as Johnny joined her.

"There was nothing wrong with the radio," he said as he came alongside her. "Must have been the station."

All of them? she started to remark, but decided against it — implying that his car wasn't as cherry as it once was would be unwise. Instead, she ignored his comment and asked, "Which row is it in ...?"

Together, the siblings meandered into the somewhat disorganized graveyard. They cast about for their father's grave while Johnny carried the wreath and Barbra made sure not to lose her footing — her heels had not been designed for soft earth any more than the gravel road.

The glooming sky and lengthening shadows chased a

tickle up Barbra's spine. The place was just so empty, so ... well, dead.

"Boy, there's no one around," Johnny observed in a low voice, as though echoing her thoughts.

"Well it's late," Barbra retorted, the surroundings getting the best of her nerves. "If you'd gotten up earlier..."

"Aw, look, I already lost an hour's sleep with the time change—"

"I think you complain just to hear yourself talk." She shoved her hands into her coat pockets just as she spotted their father's headstone. "*There* it is."

Marching over at first, Barbra's steps slowed as they approached the unkempt grave. Her heartbeat was fluttering again, and she feigned a sudden interest in a low-hanging branch as Johnny knelt to set the cross-shaped wreath in place.

"I wonder what happened to the one from last year," Johnny said. "Each year we spend good money on these things, we come out here, and the one from last year's gone."

Barbra shrugged. "Well, the flowers die and ... the caretaker or somebody takes them away."

A low thunder rumbled through the evening sky from dark clouds rolling in over the horizon. Johnny leaned back to inspect his handiwork over the rims of his glasses. "Yeah, a little spit-and-polish, you can clean this up, sell it next year." He climbed to his feet. "I wonder how many times we've bought the same one."

Ignoring him again, Barbra stepped forward as Johnny stepped back. She knelt before the grave of their father, clasped her hands, closed her eyes, and began to pray.

She heard Johnny shuffling around behind her — probably uncomfortable with her supplication, if she knew her brother. The thunder rolled again, and Barbra focused to keep her breathing steady.

Sure enough, Johnny only managed to wait a few more seconds before needling, "Hey, come on, Barb, church was this morning, huh?"

Another clap of thunder — the loudest yet — made her jump a little, but it also brought her a reprieve. Her eyes remained closed, but Johnny must have taken a moment to look around, perhaps evaluating the sky for rain; a creaky rustling also told her that he was slipping back into those driving gloves of his.

But eventually, as always, he started again. "Hey, I mean, prayin's for *church*, huh? Come on ..."

Barbra sighed, but kept her eyes shut. "I haven't seen *you* in church lately."

Johnny chuckled. "Yeah, well ... there's not much sense in my goin' to church." He paused, then asked, "Do you remember one time when we were small, we were out here?"

Oh, no ...

Johnny continued, sounding nostalgic of all things! "It was from right over there. I jumped out at you from behind a tree, and Grandpa got all excited and he shook his fist at me and he said, 'Boy, you'll be damned to hell!'"

Barbra stood then, averting her eyes. Why couldn't things ever be easy with Johnny?

Johnny chuckled again, still thankfully oblivious as to how nervous he was making her. "Remember that? Right over there ..."

Barbra walked away, heading in the general direction of the car.

"Boy," Johnny said, still musing over the tree in question, "you used to really be scared here."

"Johnny," she said, turning his name into a

chastisement. Big mistake.

Johnny locked onto the tremor in her voice like a cat onto a mouse. "Hey, you're still afraid!" He sounded all too pleased with himself.

"Stop it now!" she scolded, trying in her own way to sound like their grandfather. "I mean it!"

That was the worst thing she could have done with Johnny — all it did was egg him on. He smiled and started with that annoying, creepy voice of his. "They're coming to get you, Barbra ..."

"Stop it! You're ignorant!"

Barbra turned her back on him, but her idiot brother kept at it. He ducked around one of the larger tombstones, then pulled himself over the top like some kind of ghoul. "They're coming for you, Barbra ..." he moaned in his Karloff-wannabe voice.

Barbra stomped her way back toward the car, and Johnny followed. She hesitated just long enough to tell him, "*Stop* it! You're acting like a *child*!"

"They're coming for you ..." Johnny insisted.

Barbra scoffed with as much false courage as she could muster and continued on her way.

It was sad, really. Here they were, two supposed adults — one teasing the other like a child, and the other *afraid* like a child. Johnny could barely maintain his faux-frightened mask as the impulse to grin at her rose and fell. He looked over to his right, and Barbra followed his gaze.

An older man was shambling through the cemetery. He swayed from side to side and looked a little bedraggled, and Barbra had to wonder if he was drunk, perhaps even driven to drink by visiting a fallen loved one here in this lonely place.

"Look!" Johnny proclaimed. "There comes one of them now."

Barbra was aghast. "He'll hear you!" she admonished with a ferocious whisper.

Johnny ran up to her, taking her by the shoulders in mock fear. "Here he comes now! I'm getting out of here!"

"Johnny!" Barbra gasped as Johnny took off. He ran past the man, and Barbra's cheeks burned in humiliation. She often thought that their grandfather had been too harsh with them, but at times like this, she wondered if maybe he should've tanned Johnny's hide a little *more* often.

Her hands tucked into her pockets and her eyes low in embarrassment, Barbra continued on her way. She would cross paths with the poor man in a matter of seconds, and she prepared to apologize for her brother's boorish antics.

The man attacked her.

Barbra screamed as he grabbed at her, only the collar of her coat preventing his fingernails from tearing into the flesh of her throat. Her shrieks grew strangled as he clutched at her, pulling her toward his snarling mouth — he snapped his teeth as though trying to bite her face! Despite the wildness of his expression, he made very little noise. His body smelled horrible, and from what little sound he did make, his rancid breath made her sick.

Johnny stopped and looked back just in time to see the man assault his sister. For a moment, he could not respond — the sight was otherworldly to him. He had just been *teasing* Barbra that the man was coming to get her; for the stranger to actually be *doing* so was ... well, it was ridiculous. Outrageous. Couldn't be happening.

Barbra wailed, pulling away from the maniac with all her strength. She pounded at him, his chest and his face. When her fist came near his mouth, he again tried to bite her.

Johnny finally broke into action. He dashed back to Barbra, throwing himself against the madman and wedging his arm between them. He pulled and tugged, desperate to get the man away from his sister.

"Johnny!" Barbra cried. "Help me!"

Finally, Barbra managed to slip from the man's grasp. The lunatic grew wild in agitation, twisting around in Johnny's arms. Barbra then ceased to exist, and Johnny became the target of his fury.

Cowering against a gravestone, Barbra watched helplessly as Johnny wrestled with their assailant. The man bit and snapped at Johnny, trying to sink his teeth in wherever he could reach. Johnny cried out as the man's fingers raked down his face, pulling his glasses off and digging into his eyes. The man still made little noise, and what few sounds escaped his throat were no more coherent than those of a rabid dog.

Having his glasses ruined, of all things, inspired Johnny to his own greater violence. He grab the maniac and shoved him down with enough force to finally break his grip. When the man got right back up onto his feet, Johnny was ready for him, meeting this latest attack with one of his own. They grappled with one another, Johnny clutching and punching at the man's mid-section, while the man sank his teeth into the padding of Johnny's coat shoulder without doing any real harm. They twisted, spun, and toppled over — Johnny squirmed around, aiming to land on top so that he could press his advantage.

It didn't work.

With a sickening crack, Johnny's head and neck collided with the raised grave marker of one Clyde Lewis Myers. He twitched for two or three seconds ... and then lay very, very still.

It all happened so fast. Why, just one minute ago, certainly no more than two, she and Johnny had been bickering over their father's grave. And now—? How was this—? How could this *be*?!

Barbra gasped as the man crawled forward onto Johnny, his mouth open ...

... and it was that very sound escaping her lips which drew the creature's attention back to his original prey.

And that's what he is, a creature, *not a man, not a maniac, it's a creature, a* ghoul, *oh, God, she could see it in its eyes, they were so cold, so lifeless.*

But not entirely empty. As lightning streaked across the sky, Barbra could see *craving* in those eyes — a hunger, a wicked desire ... for *her.*

Forgetting Johnny, the man, the *creature*, clambered to his unsteady feet. His mouth moved, but not to speak. He was chewing the air, just as he wanted to chew her flesh.

They're coming to get you, Barbra.

Barbra ran. She did not think of Johnny, lying there helpless. She did not even think to call for help — who was around to hear her cries?

She just ran.

And the creature followed.

Even as she stumbled over the uneven ground, desperate to get back to the car and away from this place, she could hear it, shambling and battering its way through the low-hanging branches of the trees. It was coming, and it wasn't going to stop until it—

One of her heels sank into the soft earth, and she fell. For a moment she could only lie there, certain that the creature would fall upon her at any moment!

But no, it was still in pursuit, just not as close as she had feared. It was awkward and clumsy, and could not hope to catch her *so long as she kept moving.*

Kicking her other heal off with a flick of her foot, Barbra pushed onward, and at last reached the car.

Jerking the door open, she threw herself into the

driver's seat. She might not own a car, but she knew enough about driving to get the hell out of ...

The keys were missing.

Of course they were. The keys were in Johnny's pocket.

Johnny ...

Coming back to her senses enough to lock the doors, she moaned as the creature caught up with her. It grab the handle and yanked on it helplessly, appearing confused and frustrated that it would not open. In fact, it was *pushing* on the glass with its other hand, as though it did not quite remember *how* to open the door. Enraged, it slapped at the window with both hands, then tried to open the door again, then slapped the window, then tried the door ... it could *see* her through the glass, but could not understand why it couldn't *reach* her.

Flailing and bumbling, it ran behind the car around to the passenger door and repeated its pulling and slapping, pulling and slapping, its mouth open and chewing the air, chewing, oh, why wouldn't it stop, why wouldn't it go away?!

Suddenly, the creature's wild motion prompted it to catch sight of something behind it, something on the ground, too small or low for Barbra to see. It pushed away from the car, and for the briefest moment, Barbra thought that maybe, just maybe, it was leaving.

But then her blood ran cold as it stooped, twisted around (nearly stumbling from its lack of coordination), and returned to the car with a rock bigger than its own fist. Showing more cleverness than when it had tugged in futility at the door handle, it smashed the rock against the window once, twice ...

Barbra screamed as the rock crashed through the glass on the third impact. The creature lost its grip, and the stone missed Barbra's thigh by only the narrowest of margins.

The creature paused for a moment, requiring a second to absorb that it had, in fact, achieved its goal. Then it reawakened, dribble running from its lips as it threw itself into the open window, reaching for Barbra, reaching, dirty fingernails clawing toward her face ...

Lightheaded and desperate, Barbra looked around. If she fled the car, the creature would just clamber back out of the window and come after her on foot. It was slow and clumsy, but all it would take was another fall on her part to bring the thing down upon her like death itself.

What could she do? If only she had the keys!

Her hands were acting almost before her mind understood what she intended to do. Johnny had parked near the top of the hill, far enough over the summit that the car was angled forward. Barbra released the parking brake and pulled the gear into Neutral, then seized the steering wheel as the car began to roll.

The creature, whose long legs were still outside the vehicle, was caught off-guard. As the car rolled and picked up speed, it was dragged back out of the window. Barbra glanced over to see that it was *trying* to hold on, but it again seemed confused by the entire situation. It could not understand how or why its prey was getting away, and a last-ditch leap through the open window or climbing on top of the car were apparently beyond its comprehension.

Soon enough, the car was rolling faster than the creature could stumble to keep up, and it lost its grip. It did not give up, but continued to shamble along after her.

Barbra guided the car along the gentle curves of the cemetery road, and the creature fell further and further behind. Perhaps she would be all right after all, get away from the thing, so that she could get help and come back for Johnny.

For Johnny ...

With her immediate danger past, thoughts of her brother brought Barbra to tears.

No! She had to keep control of herself! She had to! Only she could save Johnny!

She turned to look back through the rear window, but this time she was hoping that the creature *was* still in sight, because if it gave up too soon it might remember that Johnny was still back there, unconscious and helpless. She had to make sure she lured it as far away from Johnny as possible—!

With her eyes off the road, Barbra did not see the next curve ahead. In those few seconds, the car lurched off the dirt road and ground its driver's side up against a large tree, coming to a rough halt.

If the motor had been running, it would not have mattered — the damage to the car was superficial. But since she had been coasting, the car had lost all momentum.

She was stranded, and the creature was getting closer every second.

The driver's side was pinned, so Barbra crawled across the front seat to exit out the passenger door — some of the loose, broken glass cut into her knees, but she didn't even notice. Stockinged feet crunching on gravel and dead leaves, she bolted away from the creature.

Cutting across the cemetery in the general direction of the main road, Barbra crashed through branches and twigs and underbrush, and soon her feet were just as torn up as her knees. She hoped to lose the creature this way, but she wasn't sure how much longer her exposed hands, feet, and legs could take the punishment.

Finally, after a short time that stretched an eternity for Barbra, she broke through onto the smooth dirt she had sought. Risking one glance over her shoulder, she really put on the speed now, intending to race down the road until she was safe.

Thunder rolled across the land once again, and as if on cue, the creature appeared. As feebleminded as it seemed, it had managed to cut straight across a less-wooded area, reducing the ground it had to cover by almost half. Barbra whimpered and again angled away from the road to avoid it.

In the fading light of dusk, she spotted a rundown, white farmhouse standing across an empty and overgrown field. Should she seek shelter and help there, or continue on to the main town? How far away had it been? Johnny had been driving (and bickering about the broken radio), so she hadn't been paying close attention. They'd been through here many times before, but she was so rattled!

With a glance back at the approaching creature, Barbra hurried toward the farmhouse.

She was gasping by the time she stumbled against an old gas pump near the barn. On closer inspection, she felt less hopeful that the farmhouse would be occupied — it had a feeling of *desertion* to it. Still, what choice did she have? Slow as the creature was, it never seemed to tire — she needed to get out of sight, and quickly.

Circling wide around to the front of the house (perhaps the creature would think she had run straight past it without stopping?), she climbed the stairs onto the porch before collapsing against a post in exhaustion. She wanted to call out for help, but she couldn't risk the creature overhearing her.

After giving her burning legs an all-too-brief respite, she tried the front door — *Locked*!

Nearing tears once more, she leaped from the porch to swing around toward the back of the house. The lawn was at an incline here, and she slid and fell, but was again on her feet and running in a heartbeat.

An instant before she reached the edge of the house, she caught herself — depending upon where the creature was, she might be exposing herself if she continued on! Forcing herself to move with extreme caution, she inched her way forward and peered around the corner.

No, oh no, no!

The creature was still in pursuit. It moved with less zeal now, but it was halfway across the open field, still shambling straight for her.

In renewed terror, she abandoned stealth and continued to circle the house. If the back door was also locked, she would have no choice but to press on, and she did not know how much longer her legs could ...

There! Oh, thank you, God!

A small back porch with a narrow doorway — and the door was standing open! Within the shadows, she could see a counter top, a kitchen table, and on the table, a plateful of fruit ... all so safe and reassuring in their blessed *normalcy*!

Mewling as much with relief as with fear, Barbra rushed toward the open door ...

Ben

Ben stepped off the bus and stretched the kinks out of his back. According to the schedule, he would have to wait two hours for the transfer bus to come through — at *least* two hours, as he could not count on the buses running on time out here in the middle of nowhere. Taking his jacket off, he looked around, but all he found was an old gas station, which was closed, and an eatery called Beekman's Diner. He realized that it had been a while since he had eaten, so he picked up his modest suitcase and headed into the diner.

Business was slow in Beekman's. Aside from himself, only four other people had gotten off the bus, and two of them had started walking up the road. There were a pair of old men sitting at the counter, sipping at cups of coffee and bickering over the best way to prepare catfish, and an overweight janitor sat slumped in the farthest booth with a baseball cap pulled down over his eyes.

"Wherever you want," said a tired-looking waitress, indicating the open booths. The two other travelers walked ahead of him and sat together at a booth near the middle of the small, narrow diner. Ben took the nearest booth, tossing his suitcase and jacket in beside him. It was a lot cooler in here, so he kept his sweater on as he sat down.

The waitress came to him first. "Passin' through?" she asked the obvious with no real interest in her voice.

"Yes, ma'am."

"Just coffee, or should I bring you a menu?"

"I'd like some water, and please bring me a menu."

The waitress exhaled and nodded, *almost* concealing her annoyance at the extra effort required on her part.

It did not faze Ben in the least. As a high school teacher, he had been subjected to every variety of passive-aggression under the sun — from simple eye-rolls to soul-deep sighs, Ben had seen and heard it all.

The woman brought him his menu a minute later, then perked up a bit when he ordered a very simple burger and fries. When he asked for her opinion on the best pie for dessert, she returned his warm smile with one of her own. By the time she brought his food, she was exchanging small pleasantries, albeit one sentence at a time.

Just like with so many of his students, Ben had won her over.

It didn't always work out this way, of course. Some people wore shells too tough to crack with entreaty. Ben had learned long ago that there were times for charm, and there were times to put his foot down, hard. He was glad that charm had worked here.

Ben had finished his entree and was waiting for his slice of peach cobbler when he saw the woman standing in the road.

Even after he set eyes upon her, it took him a moment to absorb the oddity of it. By now, the sun was low in the sky and the shadows were long, and the diner's tinted windows didn't help. Ben almost looked away before it struck him how ... well, how she was just standing smack in the middle of the road. She was dressed in what *appeared* to be a nurse's uniform, but even in the poor light, he could see that it was very dirty — a particularly nasty stain ran from the left side of her neck down onto her breast. Her hair was a mess, too, hanging wild and hiding much of her face.

And there she was, just standing in the middle of the

road.

"Here you go," the waitress said as she set his cobbler onto the table.

"Mmm ...? Oh, thank you, ma'am ..."

"You all right?" she asked, but then answered her own question when she followed his gaze. "Oh, my Lord!"

One of the old men turned on his stool. "What's that, Clara?"

"Look there!" the waitress exclaimed. What Ben had considered merely strange had struck a stronger chord with his server, and her voice trembled as much as her pointing finger.

Now both old men were looking out the big front windows, as were Ben's fellow bus travelers. Only the janitor remained oblivious, still snoozing away in the back booth.

"Is that Liza Connelly?" one of the men asked as he rose from his stool for a closer look.

"I, I think so, yeah," the waitress answered. To Ben, she explained, "She's my neighbor." Her fingertips were touching her quivering lower lips now. "She works as a nurse over at the county hospital. That's a ways from here."

The woman in the road, Liza, was moving now. A very slow pace, and with an awkward gait, but she was moving. Straight for the diner.

Ben did not know why this disturbed him — if anything, Ms. Connelly looked as though she might need help — but it did.

Perhaps this was why he was hesitant to stand, slow to move. He found himself reluctant to take action, which was very out of character for him. As such, it was one of the older patrons who announced, "I'll go see if she's okay." And it was the two old men together who hurried to the front door.

And so Ben watched it all happen:

The two old-timers hustled until they were about ten feet away from Liza, then they slowed down. Ben could see one of them talking to her, probably asking if she were all right.

Liza turned in their direction, but she did not look up right away; her hair was still hanging in her face.

The speaker reached out to Liza now, taking her by the arm, guiding her toward the diner.

Liza leaned toward his hand, stooped her neck ... and *bit* at him. Ben blinked in amazement, but the waitress' gasp told him that he had not imagined it — Liza had tried to *bite* the old man.

The speaker jerked back, turning into profile as he addressed his partner from the counter. Ben saw his mouth form the words, *Did you see that?* His expression was both mystified and offended.

Whatever the men might have tried next was irrelevant. Liza threw herself at the speaker, her temperament suddenly that of a wild animal.

The speaker, now the *victim*, tried to push her away, but as he shuffled backward he lost his footing. He stumbled and fell.

Liza landed atop him and bit him, bit him right on the face. Her teeth sank into his cheek and ripped the flesh away in horrifying strings of gore, exposing his gums and molars to the air.

Ben could hear the victim's screams through the glass.

The man's partner stared down at his friend, who was by now crying out for help as the crazed nurse continued her assault. The partner took a single step backward ... and then he turned and ran as fast as his old legs would carry him — up the road, away from the diner.

Ben slowly became aware that the waitress was screaming as well. Her hands were pawing at her face as though she wanted to cover her eyes, yet could not. She hopped up and down in place, but seemed unable to look away from the carnage.

One of Ben's fellow travelers whimpered and hid her eyes; her male companion hunched deeper into the booth, vomiting onto the seat.

In all the chaos, only two people maintained even a semblance of calm: Ben and the janitor, who was just now waking up, looking confused and irritated.

"Help him!" the waitress demanded, addressing either Ben or the janitor, someone, anyone. *"Help him!"*

Yes. Help him.

Ben finally moved. He slid out of the booth and looked around before finally deciding that his jacket might be the most useful tool at hand (he later cursed himself for not thinking to grab his suitcase). He seized the jacket from the seat and rushed out the front door.

The nurse, Liza, was still tearing into her victim, but the old man was barely fighting her now — his arms wrapped around her in a mockery of intimacy as her teeth sank into the side of his neck. Blood sprayed outward in a sickening arc, but the old man was past expressing his pain.

Swallowing his gorge, Ben edged around her, avoiding her line of sight and treading with a gentle step as he circled around a parked Chevy pickup truck. He could see that it was far too late to save the old man who'd had the misfortune to try and speak with a raving lunatic, but if Ben pulled this off, he could prevent her from harming anyone else.

When he was behind her hunched back, he loosened his grip on his jacket to let the torso fall free, then coiled the ends of the sleeves around his hands. With sweat dampening his forehead, Ben crept forward ... slowly ... slowly ...

At the last moment, Liza reacted as though she heard him. She cocked her head, then straightened and twisted to the side, but her movements were stiff and clumsy, which bought Ben the critical extra second he needed.

God, please don't let me miss!

Lunging forward, Ben threw his jacket over her head and wrapped it around her face. He twisted his forearms, coiling the sleeves even tighter around his wrists, and with a final cinch, closed his impromptu trap. Perfect! The crazy bitch was now blinded, half-deaf, and most important, could not bite him.

That didn't mean she wasn't still dangerous, though. She flailed about in apparent confusion at first, but as soon as she touched his hands and arms, she went wild. She bucked and thrashed, tugging at the sleeve of his sweater, trying to get free and latch onto him at the same time.

Fortunately, Ben outweighed her by forty, maybe fifty pounds. He pulled her halfway to her feet, then shoved forward with his knee in her lower back. She collapsed back to the ground, lying nearly prone this time, allowing Ben to slip a shaky arm around her throat ...

It's okay, she can't bite you through the jacket, do *it!*

... after which he applied considerable force into choking her.

It was over. In another few seconds, Ms. Liza Connelly would black out, which would allow Ben to hogtie her with his ruined jacket. They could call the local police for her, and an ambulance for the old-timer (for what good it would do), and then maybe someone could tell him just what in the hell was ...

The woman was not blacking out.

It made no sense. Not only was the jacket smothering

her face, but Ben was putting so much pressure on her windpipe, he feared he might crush something if he didn't let up soon. She *couldn't* be able to breathe through all this; despite her exertions, she wasn't making so much as a peep.

That's when Ben realized that she had made very little noise through the whole affair. Some wheezing, a little moaning ... but otherwise she had made none of the racket one would expect from someone who was so *clearly* out of her mind.

He squeezed her throat harder than ever, as hard as he could, and now he *did* feel something crumpling in there ... and yet she *still* continued to struggle.

I don't understand—

"She still goin'?"

Startled, Ben looked up to see the janitor emerging from Beekman's. The man had unscrewed a broom or mop handle and brandished it now before him. He approached the mauled old man, who by now had stopped moving altogether.

"Yeah," Ben answered after a moment. "I'm trying to knock her out."

The janitor squatted next to the old man. He started to touch his throat, then jerked his hand away from the bloody mess; he settled for touching his wrist instead. After a moment, he announced, "Joe here's dead."

Liza, rather than getting weaker from Ben's efforts, suddenly surged in her twisting and turning. She started thrashing about in the direction of the janitor's voice, evidently riled by the proximity of new prey.

"I can't knock her out," Ben said, hoping that, somehow, the janitor might offer an explanation. "She can't be breathing, I'm cutting off the blood supply to her—"

"Knock her in the head," the janitor said, releasing the old man's wrist and standing. His voice shook with anger.

"I don't want t—"

"I said knock her in the fuckin' head!"

The janitor caught Ben off guard as he rushed forward and kicked Liza, hard, right where her face would be. His boot struck closer to Ben's choking arm than he cared for, but it more than got the job done — he heard, and felt, a loud *crunch* as the nurse bucked once, then collapsed.

Ben dropped her, then stood and backed away. His right arm was aching and trembling from the exertion. "I think you just killed her, man."

"Like I give a fuck," the janitor seethed before spitting on her unmoving body. "She fuckin' killed *Joe*! Fuckin' bit his face and throat and killed him!"

"Okay, okay!" Ben said, holding up his hands and gesturing for the man to calm down. "I'm not passing judgement here, I'm just ... saying ..."

From around the corner of Beekman's appeared another woman. She was wearing a hospital gown, and even in the dying daylight, Ben could see that she, too, was a dirty mess.

First a nurse, now a patient, Ben thought. *How fitting.*

The janitor's jaw dropped a little when he set eyes on the new woman, but the instant she started walking in their direction, the anger returned. "Another one."

"Wait, now, we don't know ..." The patient's face contorted when she saw them, and she reached out with fingers hooked into claws. "Okay, it's another one."

"What the fuck is goin' on here?"

"I don't have a clue."

The patient shared some of the nurse's unsure footing, but she was moving a bit faster. She would be on them in seconds if they remained where they were.

With a gentle but firm hand, Ben touched the janitor's shoulder and pushed him back toward Beekman's door. "Let's get inside."

"To hell with that." The janitor shook free, moved forward to meet the patient halfway, then hauled back with his broomstick like a batter at the plate before swinging it around with all his might.

In his hurry and vehemence, his aim faltered. Rather than slamming the broomstick across the side of her head, it skipped off the knuckles of one of her outstretched hands. He still struck her in the face hard enough to break the broomstick in half — and to send a number of broken teeth flying through the air — but it didn't even knock her unconscious, let alone kill her.

The patient stumbled back, her jaw askew. But she made no sound, never took her eyes off the janitor. Ben was also surprised by how little blood flowed from her ruined mouth.

When a raspy moan did float through the air, it did not come from the patient. Another person — a man this time — had appeared from around the same corner. He was dressed as neither a nurse nor a patient, just plain street clothes, and he was not dirty. But it took all of two seconds for his gait, expression, and the dark circles under his eyes to reveal that he was just like the others.

"Come on," Ben urged again, "we need to get inside."

The janitor threw down his broken weapon. His failure with the patient had rattled him, and when he repeated, "To hell with that," he said it with less bluster and more dread. He backed away from the two while fishing into the pockets of his overalls. "I'm gettin' out of here." He produced a set of keys and turned toward the Chevy pickup truck parked in front of the diner.

"Wait," Ben said. "I'll get everyone else. We'll leave together."

"Fuck off. I'm goin' now."

"Just wait a second, they can climb into the back of—"

"I said fuck off! I'm not wait—*Ah*!"

The janitor had almost reached his truck, was stepping over the old man, Joe, in his rush to the driver's door. He cried out because old Joe had grab his ankle.

"Jesus Christ, Joe! I thought you were *dead*! You scared the ..."

Joe sat up, looked around ... then down at the ankle he was holding, and the leg attached to it.

"Joe?"

The old man leaned forward, just as casual as you please, and sank his teeth into the janitor's calf. Blood soaked through the pants and gushed into his mouth, some of it squirting out through the gaping hole in his cheek.

Ben's chest tightened, and he tried to reject everything that was happening, reject the whole mess. None of this made sense, so none of this could be happening — none of it!

The janitor was screaming and trying to pull away, but old Joe had his teeth sunk in deep. The janitor punched at the old man, but he did not let go.

The terrible yet engrossing scene vied for Ben's full attention, but he became conscious of a thumping to his right. He glanced over to see Clara the waitress and the male bus traveler through the front window of Beekman's, each of them pounding on the glass with one hand while pointing with the other. His wits were intact enough for him to follow the direction they indicated, but by then it was too late.

The patient with the ruined mouth and the normal-looking man both seized the janitor from behind. The patient could do little more than gnaw her ragged lips against him — she lacked her front teeth, and her jaw was no longer in alignment — but the man bit the janitor's right ear off.

All four of them — one of them struggling; three of them feeding, *feeding!* — tumbled to the ground and rolled into an atrocious jumble. The afflicted three focused all of their attention on their latest quarry.

Ben, for the moment, was forgotten.

He crept away, back toward the diner. He hated to leave the janitor to such a fate, but the actions of old Joe told him one indisputable fact.

Whatever was happening, it was *contagious.*

Ben was mere steps from the front door when he spotted the janitor's dropped keys. All in an instant, he knew what he had to do.

The woman who had traveled on the bus with him opened the door to greet him, to let him back inside as quickly and quietly as possible, but he shook his head.

"No," he whispered.

"What?" she gasped, then covered her own mouth with a frightened look at the three feeders. For now, they remained focused on the janitor.

"Get the waitress or the cook to lock this door, then shut off all the lights. Try to keep quiet."

"What about *you*?"

Ben swallowed. "I'm going for help."

The woman opened her mouth to say something, then hesitated. She stole one more peek at the three lunatics, then nodded. "Good luck," she said, and closed the door without trying to change his mind. A second later, without any help from the staff, she locked it.

He was committed now. Turning around, Ben took just a moment to build his nerve.

Would it be better do this slow or quick?

He opted for quick.   Rushing straight through the hellish chaos, he stooped long enough to snatch the janitor's keys, then jumped away before his arm or leg could be seized.

He needn't have worried. They remained focused on … on what was left of the janitor. My God, they were actually *eating* him!

don't think about that, don't stop, just keep moving, keep moving before they notice you*, damn it*

In seconds, Ben was behind the steering wheel, the door re-locked behind him. Adrenaline demanded that he get the hell out of there *now*, but he wasn't entirely sure where to go.   In his rush, he had forgotten to ask for directions — which would have required entering the diner to talk to the waitress, anyway.

Think, damn it!

Okay … okay … he knew that the two other people who has disembarked with him had started walking up the road to his right, north, away from the old gas station. When Joe's cowardly friend had taken off running, he, too, had gone in that direction. If he had to bet money on it, he would go with the direction the three locals had taken.

All right. That's it then.

But now that he was sitting inside a locked vehicle and the three sick people, or whatever they were, remained oblivious to him, he felt secure in slowing down, if just for a moment.

The biggest problem was that he had no idea what was happening. He needed *information*.

Pushing the key into the ignition, he turned it only halfway, just enough to engage the truck's battery. Ready to turn down the volume at a moment's notice, he switched on the radio.

For the first several seconds, he heard nothing but static ...

Great, just great!

... but then the instant before he twisted the knob back to Off, a male voice broke through.

"*... back on ...?*" it asked. The signal continued to whistle and scratch, but then the man continued, "*Oh ... uh, ladies and gentlemen ... we're coming back on the air after an interruption due to technical problems—*"

Thump!

Ben jerked in surprise, switching off the radio on reflex as he turned to the driver's side window.

The patient, her wretched mouth a ghastly sight up close, had left the janitor ...

Maybe because she can't eat him *very well with broken teeth and jaw?*

... and was now outside the door, staring in at him with milky, dead-looking eyes. She drew back her fist and pounded on the glass again.

Okay, enough was enough. Ben started the truck and threw it into Reverse. The truck swayed a bit as the front tires rolled back over the woman's feet, but she gave no reaction of any kind — she just staggered after him.

Ben shifted into Drive, turning around to his left. He would have to swing around into a U-turn if he wanted to head north ...

Coming from the cross-street, a large gasoline truck rounded the bend, heading straight for him. Well, not *straight* for him — the driver was weaving all over the road! Drunk, asleep, or in some kind of distress, the gas truck screamed right across the road without heeding the stop sign.

Ben slammed on his breaks to keep from hitting it broadside.

As the gasoline truck continued forward, tearing through the guardrail, Ben finally understood *why* the poor driver was behaving so. Ten, maybe fifteen people — men, women, even one child — were trailing after him, some of them dragging behind the truck, but most of them chasing after it in the awkward gait which Ben now recognized all too well.

The truck barreled toward the gas station, smashing through a low billboard, shattering the wooden sign into a million pieces and throwing the hanger-ons through the air. Seconds later, the truck ripped over one of the gas pumps.

Sparks flew and flames erupted, turning the gas truck into a rolling bonfire.

It didn't stop moving until it slammed headlong into the side of the gas station's front wall.

Instincts which had failed him earlier (and thereby saved him from the nurse) kicked into high gear, and Ben was out of the truck before he could contemplate the risk, the danger of such action. All he could think about was helping the driver.

He could hear an agonized scream coming from the gas truck. He did not know if it was the fire or those *things* which had gotten the man, but either way, it chilled Ben to the bone.

He didn't know what to do. He didn't know whether or not the truck was going to explode. He didn't know if he could save the man even if it *didn't* explode.

He did not know what to do.

The things which had been following after the truck had stopped now. They backed away, staring into the flames as though they were hypnotized, some of them holding up their arms as if to protect themselves even though the flames were a safe distance away.

They're afraid of fire, Ben realized.

Maybe he could use this to his advantage, to rescue the driver while they were held at bay. If the man from the bus could help him—

Ben turned back toward the diner, and his thoughts of seeking help stopped dead. Both the patient and the other sick man had emerged from behind the diner. He had not considered what that meant, but now he knew.

From his new vantage point further away from the building, he could see that the field behind the diner was *full* of those things, the majority wearing hospital gowns like the first patient. They had surrounded the place, and because the customers or staff had never gotten around to his suggestion of turning off the lights, he could also see that the things had somehow gotten inside — even with the tinted glass, he could see the shapes moving around through the windows.

If anyone were still alive, they wouldn't be for long.

Ben turned back to the burning truck, but there were no more screams.

He was alone.

The fire had spread to the gasoline station itself, and the flames licked high into the evening sky.

He was all alone.

He looked around. There were fifty or sixty of the things in plain view now. They just stood in place, staring at the flames ...

... until, slowly, one by one, they shifted their gaze to stare at *him*.

It was a petrifying, impious sensation. Ben might have frozen, rooted helpless to that spot, if he had not seen one thing.

The janitor was getting up. With his neck ravaged, with his ear and most of the fingers of one hand bitten off, with one leg mauled to the bone ... *the janitor was getting up*.

Ben was back in his borrowed pickup, was circling around and driving toward the parking lot before he realized what he intended to do.

The things did not move as Ben plowed the truck right through them. The janitor showed no sign of recognition or fear as Ben made a special point of crushing him.

They just stood there, staring at him. They scattered through the air like bugs, but there were no wails of fear, no cries of pain.

Ben sailed over the curb and raced into the coming night.

It was only a precious few minutes before he noticed the gas tank needle. He had not thought to check and see how much fuel the damned truck had, but he now saw that it was very near empty.

What could he do? There was no town center in sight as yet, and he sure as hell didn't want to be left stranded on the side of the road on *this* night.

In what little light of dusk remained, Ben was barely able to make out the white farmhouse standing in the middle of the field down a long, dirt driveway. A small barn stood on the other end of the property and what *appeared* to be a modest, single gas pump, most likely for refueling tractors and other equipment.

He could also make out movement in the yard, but would it prove to be *people* ... or more of those *things*?

Do I have any choice?

No, he didn't.

Turning off the main road, Ben drove toward the farmhouse ...

Tom and Judy

Tom leaned over her, his mouth opening to bite down on the flesh of her throat ...

Judy placed her fingers over his lips to stop him before he could tempt her further.

"Oh, Judy, I'm dyin' ..."

"Come on, Tommy, you're *not* dying."

"Judy, we've been together so long ... you're killin' me..." He craned his neck forward, reaching for her throat again.

"Tom, I swear, if you give me a hickey, I *will* kill you."

With a soul-weary sigh, Tom pulled away from her, straightening back into his place behind the steering wheel so that he could sulk in comfort. It was a familiar routine by now.

Tom and Judy had been dating for four years, since both of them were Juniors in high school. Though they had each left their teen years behind them, Tom often felt like a clumsy, awkward boy in the throes of puberty around her. Tonight was a recurring theme of their Sunday afternoon dates: Lunch; sometimes a movie; driving up to the top of Ridley Hill to park and "check out the view" before heading down to the lake for a swim ... followed, finally, by Tom's temptation to forego their promise to wait until their wedding night for consummation, and Judy's reminding him — always with just as much force as was needed — of her own unwavering devotion to that oath.

The real "problem," of course, was that Tom was an honest, nice guy — *too* nice for his own good, his pals were fond of telling him. He knew deep inside that if he were to press Judy, really press her on the subject, she probably would have given in by now.

But ... again, Tom was a nice guy. And he was already feeling guilty for having pushed her as far as he had this afternoon.

"Did you find out if you can get next Saturday off?" Judy asked, changing the subject with an ease that he found both endearing and annoying.

"Don't know yet, but ... probably not. Saturdays are big days at the garage."

Judy smiled. "Can't they spare you for the afternoon?"

"I'll try again. But they let me take off last month for the fair in Willard, so ..." He made a vague gesture of defeat.

She sighed in disappointment, then smiled again. "I understand."

Warmed by her mellow reaction, he caressed her cheek. "You always smile for me."

She snuggled her face against his palm. "Always."

"Do you think your folks'll be upset?"

"They'll be disappointed, sure, but Dad'll respect you for it."

Tom grinned. "Finally winnin' the old man over, huh?"

Judy giggled, then scooted back over to her side of the car. *Her* car, really, but Tom always drove. That just seemed like the proper thing to do, since he did not have a car of his own — yet. Truth be told, that was another reason he was a little reluctant to ask for Saturday off. He wanted to please Judy's father, but he really needed the work *and* the overtime that Saturdays at the garage often brought. If he could squirrel away just a few extra dollars this month, he might be able to finally make a downpayment on that used Mustang he'd had his eye on forever-and-a-day!

"Are we still going swimming?" Judy asked.

"Hmm?" he murmured, distracted by daydreams of picking Judy up in his bright red muscle car.

She gestured toward the south side of Ridley Hill, then glanced at the sun sinking lower in the west. "It's later than I thought." She giggled again, but made no direct comment on *why* it was later. "Do you still want to head down to the lake?" And her big smile told him that she was hoping for a Yes.

Tom glanced at his watch. "Sure, Smiley, why not?" Thoughts of muscle cars had failed to relieve the pressure in his groin, but a cold dip in the lake just might do the trick. Unless Judy brought her bikini instead of her one-piece, in which case he was in even more trouble.

As Tom started the engine and turned around to drive back down the hill, he spotted some thunderheads creeping across the horizon. Between the late hour and the possibility of rain, he might have voted to cancel their swim after all, but he didn't want to disappoint Judy.

Without even thinking about it, he reached over and turned on the radio. But instead of music, all that came out of the speakers was static.

"That's funny," Judy commented. She reached out to try another station.

"Give it a second," Tom suggested, "maybe it's just warmin' up or something. Has it given you any problems before?"

"No, not really."

"Huh ..."

They drove in silence for a minute, Tom navigating around toward the lake. He was watching the road, so it was Judy who spotted the commotion. "Something's going on over there."

"Where? By the lake?"

"Yeah ..." She squinted, then said, "It looks like they're pulling somebody out of the water. I hope he's all right."

"Me, too."

The radio static flared louder, then ceased altogether. *"Is that it? You got it?"* they heard the diskjockey say, his voice muffled as though he were facing away from the microphone.

Tom and Judy exchanged a confused glance. Something about that unprofessional snippet, the shaken tone of the man on the air, seemed somehow ... eerie.

"Uh, ladies and gentlemen, we apologize for these interruptions ... we are, uh, we're experiencing technical difficulties with the power here ... again, we apologize and will continue to, well, we'll try to remain on the air as long as possible ..."

"Tommy, what is this?" Judy asked.

He shook his head. "Don't know."

"If you're just tuning in," the diskjockey said, *"it is vital that you pay close attention. According to reports from all over the county, and some are now coming in from the entire tri-state area, we are experiencing an epidemic of unexplained mass-murder."*

The proclamation was so unexpected, so outrageous, that Tom actually laughed out loud. "What?!" he guffawed.

"Shh!" Judy leaned forward in her seat.

"What we first dismissed as hysteria can no longer be denied. We have confirmed the accuracy of many of these reports with local police and sheriff departments; the murders are real, and they are taking place as we speak. We—" Another burst of static overwhelmed the man's

voice. A second later they caught one more word — Tom thought it might have been "safety" — and then the speakers settled down to the softer static they had first heard, with no transmission coming through.

"Tom, what was *that*?" Judy asked, her voice stringent.

"A joke, honey, it had to be."

"They don't joke about stuff like that on the radio."

"Sure they do!" he laughed, but it sounded forced even to his own ears. "Remember last April Fools' Day? They talked about—"

"It's not April Fool— Oh, my God."

Having been distracted by the bizarre announcement on the radio, Tom hadn't realized that they had reached the lake. Now that they were closer, they could see that a man had, in fact, been dragged from the water and was now lying unconscious (or worse) on his back while a woman tried to resuscitate him.

"Do you think they need help?" Judy asked.

"Not sure what we can do," Tom said, but she was already opening the passenger door before they'd rolled to a complete stop. Sighing at how this day was turning out, Tom put the car in Park and got out with her.

A handful of people, all in swimwear, were standing around the drowned man, fidgeting with the same indecision Tom felt. The guy was overweight, with a *huge* gut and barrel chest, and Tom couldn't help wondering if the woman's pumping on his chest was at all effective.

"Come on, Gerald!" she shouted. "Wake up! Breathe! Please breathe!" She moved to his head, pinching his nose and blowing into his mouth.

"What happened?" Judy whispered to a teenage boy when they got close enough.

The boy shrugged. "Mister Levin just started screaming out there in the water." He gestured, listless.

"Guess he got a cramp or somethin'. Went under the water before anyone could reach him. Wasn't moving by the time his wife brought him in." Then he added with pride, "I helped her drag 'im out of the water."

"Has anyone gone for help?" Tom asked.

"Yeah, I think so." He gestured again, back the way from which Tom and Judy had just arrived.

Tom started to point out that he'd seen no car pass them by ... but then, he'd been so distracted by the "mass-murder" thing on the radio, he might've just missed it, somehow.

The drowned man's wife stopped blowing into his mouth and went back to pumping on his chest. She was crying now, but didn't let up. "Come on, Gerald. Don't be so goddamn stubborn, now. Wake up!"

Judy reached out and took Tom's hand. He clasped it back out of habit, but his attention was focused elsewhere.

None of the others were paying it any mind, but Tom's eyes were drawn to a hideous wound on Mister Levin's left calf. It was down toward the ankle, and since he was lying on his back, it wasn't all that visible, but it looked like a *chunk* had been taken right out of him, like the world's worst dog bite! It might explain why he started screaming and then drowned in the first place, but for the life of him, Tom couldn't think of what might cause such a wound in this lake. What, did someone stock it with *piranha* or something?

A long, dark trail of blood slithered from the man's calf back out into the water. Somehow, that turned Tom's stomach more than his obstructed view of the wound itself.

Then Mister Levin's hand twitched, followed a moment later by his jaw clenching.

"Oh, thank God!" his wife cried. A couple of people applauded, including Judy. "But you have to *breathe*,

Gerry! Spit that dirty ol' lake water out for me."

Switching back to his head, she leaned in to puff more air into his lungs. As she did, her husband kicked his legs once, then lifted one arm up and around his wife's neck, as if to hug her ...

Then *she* started screaming.

Everyone jolted, but no one moved or even said anything — no one had any idea what the hell was going on!

The woman tried to pull back, her screams muffled and gurgling. Even though her husband's arm fell away easily enough, she couldn't seem to straighten up at first. And when she finally did, Tom wished she hadn't.

She threw herself back, falling over onto her butt, still screaming. Her mouth was a horrid, bloody mess.

Her husband had bitten her lips off.

Tom's heart shot into his throat, and Judy's hand clamped down like a vice on his bicep.

Good God, he wasn't *really* seeing this, was he? *Was he*?

"Holy *shit*!" the teenage boy cried, and similar sentiments erupted from everyone present. Another boy, this one around ten years old, turned white as a sheet and a dark stain of urine spread out across the front of his denim cutoffs.

The wife's upper lip was almost entirely gone; her lower lip hung loose down her chin, dangling like a worm from a fishhook. She held her hands up to her face but fell short of actually touching the shocking injury.

She kept screaming, but not for long. Her husband sat up, his big gut jutting outward like a squeezed pillow, then flailed over onto his wife's legs and started chewing into her thigh.

She cried out for help, but everyone scattered in all

directions. Tom took one step forward even though he had *no idea* what he should do — his brain was still catching up with what his eyes were telling him — but Judy clamped down on his arm again.

"Tom!" she pleaded. "We have to get out of here!"

"But, the woman ... she ... *lips*!" He knew it was incoherent, but it was all he could get out.

"No, Tommy, *look*!"

He looked at her first, then followed her pointing finger.

A woman was staggering out of the lake, a blue, bloated woman who looked as though she had been under the water for far too long. Clad in a tattered swimsuit, her arms were outstretched, reaching for them — her skin was decrepit, her eyes were cloudy, and part of her nose had been chewed away.

Tom took Judy by the hand, and they ran for the car.

But they didn't get very far.

A man in a filthy hospital gown stood next to Judy's car. He was standing on the driver's side, peering in through the window. His back was to Tom and Judy, and Tom could see through the flap of his gown, which was only held together by a single threadbare tie at this point, that the man had dried shit running down each leg — he had soiled himself, but hadn't bothered to clean it up.

Tom stopped so abruptly that Judy collided with him. She squealed — she had been looking over her shoulder at the woman from the water — and cut herself off when she saw the problem.

The man wasn't aware of them, yet. He was just staring into the car, as though admiring it, maybe considering it for purchase. If it weren't for the gown and his state of uncleanliness, Tom would've had no idea anything was wrong.

"What do we do?" Judy whispered into his ear, her voice trembling.

Thunder echoed from the dark clouds Tom had seen earlier. The man glanced up for a brief moment, then returned his attention to the car. He hadn't reacted to any of the other people as they ran screaming in all directions, fleeing in their own vehicles or on foot ... so *maybe* he would ignore them, too? Maybe they could circle around to the other side of the car, then slip in through the passenger door?

A moan wheezed out of the man. He raised his left hand — Tom could see the hospital bracelet — and pressed his palm against the car window. That was all he did, it wasn't even threatening, really ... but something about it crushed any thought of trying to sneak past him and into the car.

Tugging Judy in another direction, Tom led her away and, thankfully, the man never realized they were there.

When they had put a respectable distance between themselves and the soiled man, Judy asked again, "Tom, what are we going to *do*?" He could tell she was near tears, but trying to keep a brave face for him.

Tom didn't know. As the minutes passed, he was finding the whole situation *harder* to process, to deal with. He hadn't thought before, he'd reacted — to the drowned man, to the bloated woman, to the soiled man ... all a very simple, very easy *Stay the hell away from them!*

But now ... now he was running through the fields north of the lake with his girlfriend, running from the most bizarre threats he could ever have imagined, it looked like rain, it would be getting dark soon, and they had lost their car.

"Tom—!" she started again, panting as she strove to keep up with him.

"I'm *thinkin'*, honey!" he replied, his tone a little sharper than he had intended.

Judy held her peace, but she fell further and further behind him as they ran, until Tom had to choose between slowing down or leaving her. He slowed down.

"Tommy," she told him between gulps of air, "I'm scared."

"Me, too."

"We can't keep running like this. Where are we going?"

He shook his head. "Don't know yet. It'll take us too long to get back to town on foot, not with those ... those weird people runnin' around."

God, he thought, prayed, *did she really come right out of the water like that? Was that real?*

Thunder sounded again, and Judy insisted, "We need to call our folks, Tommy."

"There's ..." He looked around. "There's that old farmhouse not too far from here. Remember? I pointed it out to you last Thursday when we were lookin' for—"

"I remember," she nodded.

"I *think* the old lady still lives there. It might be worth a shot. Then we could maybe borrow her phone."

"Do you really think so, Tom?"

He opened his mouth to answer, and that's when he saw the man wandering through the field about a hundred yards away from them. That's all he was doing, just wandering around, but after the outlandish things Tom had just seen, he was very sensitive to the man's lurching, unsteady stride. He didn't know what it meant, but he sure as hell didn't like it.

Squeezing Judy's hand tighter, he said, "We don't have a choice, honey. We've gotta go. Right now."

Tom struck out for the farmhouse, and Judy followed ...

THE COOPERS

"We're lost."

"No we're not."

"We are *lost*, Harry."

"No, we are *not*. I know what I'm doing, Helen."

Helen Cooper shrugged. "Fine. Just make sure we have some place to stay before it gets dark."

Then she and her husband, Harry Cooper, lapsed into another cold silence.

In the backseat, their daughter, Karen, quietly read her adventure book and made no comment, no "Are we there yet?" or "I have to go the bathroom" or any of the other outbursts a normal 10-year-old would be prone to after hours of riding in a car.

Karen knew better. She knew her father, recognized his moods. She could tell from his tone of voice alone that her mother was right, that they *were* lost and he *knew* it, but would never admit it. So she remained still, calling no attention to herself, and read her book ... even though she *did* kind of have to go to the bathroom.

Helen glanced over her shoulder, as though sensing her daughter's discomfort. Karen met her gaze and smiled — Helen smiled back, and apologized with her eyes. Her sweet little girl shrugged and went back to her reading.

Helen sighed under her breath and turned her eyes back to the road and the empty, rural setting on either side of it. She asked herself for the thousandth time: Is this *really* what's best for Karen?

Helen and Harry Cooper had decided some time ago

that they no longer wanted to be married.   They each claimed to still *love* one another, they just didn't particularly *like* one another anymore — Harry felt that Helen had gotten too "uppity" and aloof; Helen felt that Harry's less-than-impressive height and premature hair-loss had made him too aggressive and antagonistic. But Harry's parents had gotten divorced while he was in his teens and Helen's had done the same while she was still in elementary school, so they had discussed the matter and chosen to remain together for Karen's sake, at least until she had graduated high school and moved on to her own life.   It was a choice that many parents made, but she was learning for herself why it was an unpopular one.   Karen wasn't fooled, not for a minute, so what was the point?

"Is that ...?" Harry asked in a low voice, then muttered even lower, "Shit."   He had spotted a couple of buildings, had probably hoped that one was a motel ... but no, they were just a diner and closed gas station.   Helen wanted to point out that the occupants of Beekman's Diner might be able to provide them with directions, but she saved her breath — if Harry thought it was his *own* idea, he might consider it, but not if she suggested it.

But no, they passed through the three-way intersection and kept going.   Helen rolled her eyes and stared out her side window.   So long as Harry found a place for them to stay before it got dark, she didn't really care.

To be fair, it was partly her fault, anyway.   She and Karen were only in this mess because she had opted to be nice to Harry and do him a favor.

Harry's annual sales convention had been held over this weekend — checking into the hotel on Friday evening; checking out on Sunday afternoon.   While Harry had been too proud to come right out and ask her, he had dropped numerous hints about how it would "look better" for him if his entire family attended this year. Sure, it was boring as hell, but Karen had always been a well-behaved little girl, and if Harry came across as a successful "family man," it would impress his more conservative associates. Maybe make for a bonus, or even a promotion, this coming holiday season.

So after a few days of these hints and comments — and as Harry's attitude threatened to edge into passive-aggressive sulking — Helen had "suggested" that maybe she and Karen should come along, too. Harry had been very pleased, and for the remaining weeks leading up to the sales convention, he had been almost cheery for a change.

When the weekend in question arrived, they had packed their Sunday best and driven down. The hotel was a little more expensive than expected, as had been the food and other amenities which his company was apparently *not* picking up this year, but Harry had maintained at least a neutral posture throughout.

The problems had started when Sunday morning rolled around, and it had become clear that having his family along hadn't made quite the impression that Harry had been hoping for — no mention of bonuses, or promotions, or even new clients. Harry began to drop new hints that it was somehow *Helen's* fault, that she had come across as too snooty, too cold ... and she'd had the audacity to look better than his boss' wife.

Helen just gritted her teeth and took it. At least he wasn't trying to blame Karen, and she wanted to spare her daughter from witnessing an all-out slugfest between her parents.

They had checked out of the hotel early, and Harry got it in his head that he knew a shortcut that would shave some time off their return trip. Helen had her doubts, but the truth was that Harry had made this trip more often than she, knew these roads better than she, so she kept her mouth shut ... until it was too late.

They'd gotten a little turned around almost immediately, but Harry refused to admit it, so they didn't backtrack when it would've been easier. He wanted to save time, so they kept going. And going. And as they got more and more lost by mid-afternoon, it became clear to Helen that they'd never reach home tonight. Harry's big plan had not only failed to save time, it was going to *cost* them another night in some motel.

Helen enjoyed that little victory in private.

"Now what the hell is this?" she heard Harry grumble.

She looked back to the road. Ahead of them, two small cars had had what appeared to be a minor collision, a fender-bender that shouldn't have resulted in any injuries. What was odd, though, was the sheer number of people surrounding the cars. It had to be at least a dozen, maybe more — too many to have been squeezed into the two little vehicles.

"Lookie-loos, I guess," she commented.

"What's a 'lookie-loo', Mommy?" Karen asked from the back.

"An assho—" Harry answered, but cut himself off in mid-swear. "A jerk with too much time on his hands." He raised his voice, "Come on!" and honked the horn twice as they approached the cluster, which was blocking well over half of the road.

None of them paid any attention. Harry had to come to a full stop, and he honked the horn again, longer this time. And the people still ignored him — they were too fascinated with the interiors of the two cars from the collision.

Maybe Helen had been wrong. Maybe the people inside were hurt after all, and these witnesses were trying to help.

"Oh, for fuck's sake," Harry snarled, throwing the car into **Park**.

"Harry!" Helen snapped, appalled by his using such language in front of Karen.

But Harry didn't pay her any mind. He opened his car door, practically kicked it open, and got out.

"Just go around them, Harry," he heard Helen whine just as he closed the door, but he didn't pay any attention to that, either. He had been trying to control his temper for a while — not an easy task, what with Helen's endless nagging, but he had tried for Karen's sake. So in a way, he was glad for this obstruction. Sure, he could just go around, but then he wouldn't be able to blow off some steam.

"All right, *all right*," he declared, just short of shouting. "There's been a little accident, what a sight, we're all impressed. Now could some of you please move your asses out of our way?"

The group of people *still* ignored him. What in the hell where they doing, anyway? He couldn't see exactly, there were too many of them, but from the car closer to him, he heard ... what was that? Smacking? What was going on here, a goddamn gum-chewing contest?!

As he stomped over, his short legs pumping, Harry failed to notice the haphazard way these people were dressed. A few of them wore the expected rural outfits, suitable for farmers who didn't know the first thing about *real* job pressure, about having to meet quotas every month, about keeping your money-sucking wife in the latest fashions, about having so much fucking stress in your life that your hair starts falling out!

So it was only the very fringes of Harry's distracted mind that noted something that Helen was just starting to absorb from her viewpoint in the car — several of these people were wearing hospital attire, for staff and patients alike. And ... was that *blood*?

What exactly was going on?

But again, Harry was too perturbed to notice this on any meaningful level, so he walked right up and grab one of the women by the arm, and not gently. Tugging her away from whatever the hell was going on in there, Harry started, "Look, idiot, why don't you and your buddies—"

The woman tottered around on shaky feet, giving Harry a good look at her.

"Aah!" Harry blurted, letting go of her arm and stumbling back.

The woman's face was a bloody mess from the nose down. It reminded Harry, of all things, of the way people looked after competing in a pie-eating contest, the kind where their arms are tied behind their backs and they have no choice but to shove their faces right into the tin. But this wasn't blueberry or apple or any other pie Harry had ever heard of — if he hadn't known better, he would've sworn ... but no, surely not ...

The woman stared at him, her eyes looking murky and jaundiced. She opened her mouth wide, revealing more gore to turn Harry's stomach, and made a gurgling sound in the back of her throat.

Harry didn't like that sound, not one bit. He took another step away from her.

The woman made the sound again, reaching up with hands that were as sanguinary as her face, and others in the group reacted, rising up and out of the car to turn and stare at Harry. And they were all, all of them, were ... were ...

Harry spun on his heel and ran back to the car. He could see Helen staring behind him in shock and disbelief, her wide eyes showing too much white all the way around.

As he jumped back behind the wheel, she didn't ask any questions, she just said, "Harry, get us out of here!"

For once, the two of them were in complete agreement.

Without bothering with his seatbelt, Harry threw the car into Reverse, stomping down on the accelerator and sending the tires into a squealing fury.

Alarmed, Karen asked, "What's going on, Daddy?"

"Be still, honey," Helen replied, not wanting her daughter to get a look at the gore-splattered insanity out—

Thunk!

The car had just started building some real speed when they were jarred from the rear. Both the Coopers had been so fixated on the people in front, they hadn't bothered looking behind them.

"Oh, my God, Harry," Helen said, one hand covering her mouth. "Did you just *hit* someone?"

They both turned in their seats, their faces close together as they looked out the back window. They had indeed hit not just one, but *two* people. But any distress they would normally have experienced was warped by the sight of their victims, both of whom were men, both of whom wore doctor's greens, and both of whom were missing parts of their anatomy — one was missing his arm from the elbow down, the other missing one of his eyes and part of his cheek. Neither of them seemed to be in any pain as they flailed and tried to rise from where they had bent over the Coopers' trunk, but they did appear enamored by the sight of the Coopers looking at them, and reached out just as the woman had reached for Harry.

"God, Harry," Helen whispered, touching her husband's arm for comfort without realizing she was doing so, "what's *wrong* with these people?"

"I ... I don't know," he admitted.

Then he went into action once more. He shoved the

car back into Drive and floored it, turning the steering wheel to go around the two collided cars, something he should have done all along.

But now the group had spread out, covering even more of the road than they had before. He turned wide, trying to go around them, and the tires on his side went off the shoulder of the road, spinning in the gravel and dirt, losing any real traction.

"Harry—!" Helen cried as those insane people slammed into the passenger side of the car. They were all moving as though drunk, but the two that reached them rapidly became four, then seven, then it seemed the whole dozen or more were against the side of their car, pawing at the window and slapping at the roof and hood and trunk.

Karen screamed. So did Helen. And though he might've denied it later, so did Harry.

The car lurched, almost made it through ... and then it rocked up onto just the driver's-side tires. The engine roared in protest and dirt flew everywhere. Harry heard a strange *Whump!*, and realized it was probably the sound of one of those people reaching right into the wheel well and losing a hand or arm for their trouble.

Then the car rolled over.

Harry got the worst of it, never having refastened his seatbelt. He reached up to catch himself, but his forehead still banged up against the roof, sending stars across his vision. Helen and Karen had their belts on, but the whole experience was so unexpected and terrifying that they cried out along with him.

The car ceased rolling as it settled onto its roof, but it continued sliding down the slope away from the road, but also away from those maniacs. The noise was surprisingly loud, and the windshield cracked as something raked across it, a rock or pipe — Harry wasn't sure.

The important thing was, by the time the car stopped, they had gained a respectable distance from the mob, whose inebriated stride was making it difficult for them to follow down the slope off the side of the road. They stumbled and fell and tripped each other — Harry could see that much as he crawled onto his hands and knees — but it wouldn't take them long to catch up.

"Helen!" he asked. "You all right?"

"I ..." she looked around at him from where she hung upside-down. "I think so ..."

"Then move your ass," he ordered, keeping an eye on those things as best he could. "We've got to get out of here. Help me with Karen."

Karen was crying— no, *wailing* at the top of her lungs, and Harry didn't blame her.

After some struggling, they managed to get their daughter free of her seatbelt and pushed her out on Helen's side. Those people, those *things*, were way too close now.

"You go, Helen," he said in a moment of uncharacteristic chivalry. "Go, hurry!"

Helen crawled out — grabbing her *purse* out of habit, the silly woman! — then reached back in to help Harry.

"We've got to run," Harry was saying as he struggled to get out, "we've got to get the hell—"

Then the pitch and tone of Karen's wailing skyrocketed; she was *howling* now, but Harry couldn't see why.

"Oh, *God!*" Helen cried, her helping hands disappearing just as Harry tried to get to his feet. "Stop! Stop that, you *bitch*!"

Harry finally floundered up to a standing position, and his eyes bulged when he saw what was happening.

It was the same woman, the one Harry had grab before. She was the one who had reached into the wheel well, the one whose arm had twisted into an impossible knot as it snapped in a hundred places and wrapped around the rim of the tire, which had served to drag her along with them as the car slid off the side of the road ... and the one who had snared Karen by the wrist, then dragged his daughter closer and sank her teeth deep into the little girl's right arm.

Without thinking about it, Harry punched the woman in the face as hard as he could, with everything he had in him. The result was both sufficient and disturbing: It made her let go of Karen, which was what he had hoped for, but he felt a cold chill run down his spine as the woman otherwise ignored the blow — her nose was smashed flat, a bloody, pulpy mess that now matched the gore around her mouth ... but she didn't cry out, didn't even blink. Her head had rocked back, that was the only reason Helen had been able to pull Karen's arm free, but the woman showed no pain at all as she tugged at Karen again, trying to pull her in for another bite.

Helen screamed, "*Let go! Let go of my baby!*" She reached down, grab the woman's fingers from where they encircled her daughter's wrist, and bent them back until they broke with an audible *snap* — Harry might've been shocked by Helen's brutality, but under the circumstances, he applauded it.

The woman let go of Karen, but she *still* showed no pain, reaching out with her mangled hand as though nothing had happened.

They had no time to deal with Karen's injury — the others were so close they could almost touch the trunk of the car. Harry gathered Karen up into his arms, and the Coopers ran, ran as fast as they could.

They cleared away from the car and outdistanced their insane attackers with relative ease. But Karen was like a dead weight in Harry's arms, and in short order he was forced to slow down.

"Where are we going, Harry?" Helen asked, as out of breath from fright as from running.

"I ... don't know ..." he panted.

"Should we ... should we go back to that diner we passed?"

He shook his head. "I'll ... never make it ... that far ..."

A keening sound escaped Helen's lips, but before it could overwhelm her, she stopped and pointed. "There!"

Harry stopped as well, grateful for the rest. "Where?"

"There! Across the field!" She was pointing at an old farmhouse.

"I don't know ..." he said. "I wish we ... could get further away ..."

Thunder rolled across the land. Helen looked at Harry.

"Fine," he said. "We'll check it out ... here, help me with her, damn it — she weighs a lot more than your *purse*!"

After adjusting Karen (who was now silent and sucking her thumb like a girl half her age) in Harry's arms, the Coopers cut across the field toward the old farmhouse ...

Night

Barbra threw herself through the open back door of the farmhouse, her stockinged feet sliding on the linoleum as she seized the door and slammed it shut. She gasped in fear when it wouldn't seem to close, then sobbed in relief as she finally locked it behind her. Her jellied muscles near collapse, she sagged against the door, trembling like a leaf. With the creature no longer in sight, behind the barriers of perceived safety, her mind was already seeking denial. She wanted nothing more than to curl into a ball and go to sleep and pretend that none of this had ever happened.

But ... where was she, really?

Turning around, she realized that denial was a luxury she could not yet indulge. This house, this strange farmhouse, was very dark now that the light of dusk had been cut off. She had no idea where the homeowners were, and was hesitant to call out. And what did it mean that the back door had been standing open?

Still shaking and unsteady on her feet, Barbra forced herself to look around.

Stepping through the nearest open doorway, she found herself in a large area that was probably a living room, with a sofa, chairs, an old piano, and a medium-sized dining table in one corner. The dim light coming through the windows revealed nothing helpful, save that she was alone for now.

Or was she?

A fresh chill sent her scurrying back into the kitchen. Biting her lip in an effort to remain silent, she cast about for something, anything she could use as a weapon to defend herself.

Keeping a close eye on the as-yet-unscouted doorway, she scuttled forward to an open drawer and fished inside for what she wanted, shoving aside forks and spoons and butter knives until ...

Yes! Her fingers finally closed on the wooden handle of a butcher's knife. Pulling it free from the other silverware, she clutched it to her chest with both hands as she slumped against the refrigerator, feeling the slightest bit safer.

But she couldn't fully relax until she confirmed that she was, in fact, alone in the house. Or, God willing, maybe she could even find a phone! Her poor brother was still out there, helpless, *depending* on her to save him — she had to summon help!

Forcing herself to keep moving, Barbra advanced toward the kitchen's other open doorway.

But upon entering the smaller room, Barbra hesitated. Laying on the floor was the remains of a broken lamp. Just that — a broken lamp, very mundane; under normal circumstances, she might've just *Tsk*'ed the lazy person who failed to clean up their mess. But this evening ...

Clutching the knife tighter, she pressed onward. If only it weren't so *dark* ... but she was too afraid to turn on any lights. They would set the windows aglow, and that thing outside would know immediately where she was. But how long could she continue to wander around in the ever-darkening house before—

Sure enough, she sidled too close to one of the walls, and her hip knocked an open magazine off a piece of furniture. Its soft *ka-thunk* was terribly loud to her ears, but although she froze for a moment, no other sounds followed.

Treading carefully around the remains of the lamp, she continued onward.

Moving through a brighter hallway, Barbra peered around, then continued into the darkest room yet. Her eyes struggled to adjust back and forth, and still her ears detected nothing other than her own hushed footsteps. Maybe she was being too paranoid? The creature would surely have made noise if it had entered the house. If she hurried, if she found a phone, Johnny would have a much better—

Teeth! Gaping, huge teeth, the lips curled back as the open mouth reached for her

Barbra's heart skipped a beat, but shame and embarrassment silenced her gasp before it escaped. She had stumbled upon the homeowner's study, and what she had seen in the gloom was nothing more than the stuffed head of a warthog or some similar animal. Other heads, mostly bucks and does, were mounted on the walls — nothing more than a hunter's trophy room.

You've got to get a hold of yourself, Barbra.

Easier said than done. She could feel herself slipping, and she didn't like it. Not one bit.

It didn't help matters that even as she eased forward once more, she finally heard real movement. Blessedly, it was coming from outside, but any relief she felt evaporated when she peered through the nearest window to see that the creature had finally reached the house.

The filthy thing was leaned up against the very post where she had seized a brief respite before finding her way into the house. The creature shoved away, shuffling and weaving back and forth in its bumbling manner. It was looking at and all around the house, once again behaving as though it didn't quite understand, as if it didn't remember what a house *was*. It just wanted its prey, that was all it seemed to think about, and as its gaze raked across the window—

Barbra huddled against the wall, peeking out from around the curtain as she followed the creature's movement.

The creature stumbled around the side of the house and managed to tangle itself in the clothesline. It flailed about, yanking the lines free and ripping the support pole from the ground before throwing it against the house. It clasped at the remaining lines and tore at them, tore at them as it would surely tear at her throat!

Barbra shoved the curtain across the window and turned away, her breath short and her eyes wild. She was slipping ... slipping ...

Then her gaze fell upon the very thing she most wanted to see: A telephone!

Nearly melting in relief, she threw herself across the study, seizing the handset and dialing for the operator with shaking hands. She glanced out the study's other window, ducking down to make sure the creature didn't spot her while she was so close to rescue.

Several seconds elapsed before she absorbed that she was hearing only a weird, electronic warble.

No. Oh, no, no no no

Tears of defeat welling up in her eyes, she slammed her fingers repeatedly against the cradle, then tried dialing the operator once more. Nothing.

Slipping ... slipping ...

Shaking the handset in pitiful frustration, she slammed it down and shoved herself away from the useless piece of junk to keep from screaming at it. She was nearly out of the room before a cold hand of realization tightened around her heart and sent her scurrying back to retrieve the butcher knife.

Returning to the living room, Barbra caught a glimpse of movement through another of the many windows. She ducked, not trusting the gloom of the house to protect her from being spotted, and rushed forward until she slid onto her knees in front of the table beneath the window and, carefully, peeked over the windowsill.

The creature was visible yet again, staggering about and ogling the house with that blank expression on its face. That, in a way, was almost worse than its look of animalistic hunger when it attacked her in the cemetery — that *nothing* in its eyes!

But as disturbing as it was, Barbra soon spotted something far worse.

Behind the creature, Barbra could barely make out two people wandering up to the house! For the briefest flicker of an instant, she was torn between relief that help had arrived and horror that the creature would set upon the newcomers before she could warn them ... but then the flicker passed. Something about their gait immediately set Barbra back on edge. Although not exactly the same as the creature's, their movement was *off* in its own way, sluggish and ungainly.

Oh, no ... oh, God, please no, no ...

The creature turned around, saw the two people, took one step toward them ...

No, no, please, God, this can't be happening!

... then dismissed them, turning back to the house even as the newcomers ambled up behind it, as though joining its ranks.

Barbra shoved herself away from the window so hard she stumbled, nearly knocking over one of the dining table chairs. She fumbled to right it before it could fall over, and her shaking hands nearly made it worse. When the chair thankfully settled, she ran, ran, away from the window, away from those things, away, away ...

Back in the hallway, Barbra struggled to maintain *some* level of control. She would accomplish nothing, would be no closer to rescuing her poor brother if she collapsed, hyperventilating in the dark like a helpless child.

They're coming to get you, Barbra ...

SHUT UP, JOHNNY! I'M TRYING TO FIND HELP FOR YOU!

She stumbled yet again, this time catching herself on the bannister—

A bannister! Yes, the farmhouse had a second floor, she had seen that from outside! Up, that's where she needed to go, up and away from those things. From upstairs, she could peer down through the windows without their seeing her in return, maybe she would even find another phone, one that worked!

Up, she would go up.

But disappointment had been her constant companion since the attack in the cemetery, and this proved no different. She had barely climbed two of the stairs before catching a glimpse of something above her, something on the landing. She couldn't make out what it was, but just as she had almost immediately labeled the newcomers outside as a threat, that same warning screamed in the back of her mind now.

Stretching out her arms to either side, supporting herself between wall and bannister, she ascended the stairs at a very slow, very timid pace. Halfway up, she could finally see what waited for her ... and yet her mind couldn't accept what she was seeing. She knew what it looked like, but no ... surely it wasn't ...

But it was. It was a body. A corpse. But that wasn't what finally ripped a scream from her reluctant lips.

The person — a man? a woman? she couldn't tell —

had been mutilated. The face had been ripped to shreds as though eaten by some savage animal. The teeth were exposed where an upper lip should have been, drawn into a sickening rictus like a perverted smile. Drying, nearly black blood had congealed in the hair, hiding whatever natural color it had once been and leaving an apparent gap through the left temple and down into the brain cavity itself. The right eye was missing, but the left eye gaped its wild view upon the world, the eyelid torn, ripped, *chewed* away, leaving it staring into space. Staring at Barbra.

Something had eaten its face, and it was staring at her.

Too much. She was no longer sliding out of control. Control was gone, evaporated, her mind snapped.

Down the stairs, folding over the bannister to empty her belly, unable to find even that relief, running, running, the knife staying in her hand only by chance, through the hallway, through the dining room, to the foyer, to the front door, clawing at it, unlocking it, no thoughts of the creature or creatures outside, no thoughts at all save one faint echo, the mere glimmering of a true thought: *Johnny's the lucky one.*

The front door finally opening for her, she shoved the screen door aside as she burst into the night ...

... and into blinding light.

Bedazzled, Barbra collided with the porch post, which was all that kept her from taking a face-dive into the front yard. She heard a metallic *slam* from beyond the twins beams which struck a familiar chord, but she was beyond making sense of things. She reeled back, throwing her arms before her eyes to block the glare that threatened to excecate her.

Was she in Hell? Was *that* why she couldn't get away from horror after horror?

Then a shape stepped forward to block the

headlights—

(Headlights! That's what they were — headlights!)

—and she could see again. But would this prove any better?

She and the man in the sweater stared at each other, appraising. Barbra took another step back, but just as she had instinctively withdrawn from the previous two newcomers, something told her that this man was *not* a threat. For one thing, he was *studying* her with a leery-but-thoughtful expression in his eyes — not at all like the empty hunger of the thing that had chased her from the cemetery.

Speaking of ...

The creature had found its way around to this side of the house, and the man heard it. He looked over his shoulder, tensing. Barbra noticed, in a distant manner, that he carried a tire iron, and was poised to use it. Then he looked at Barbra again, hesitated, and instead of facing off with the creature, he pushed her back into the house. She resisted a little — hadn't there been something in the house from which she had been desperate to escape? She couldn't remember anymore. She ... she couldn't *think* anymore.

Johnny ...

Ben slammed the door shut and locked it, relaxing — just a little — for the first time since his flight from Beekman's Diner. He didn't know who this young blonde woman was, but all he cared about was that she was *normal*. A little stunned, maybe, but he could live with that — he would take whatever help he could get tonight.

"It's all right," he told the whimpering girl.

She just stared at him, as though waiting for him to do something.

Turning his back to the door, Ben looked around the

dark house. He gripped the tire iron he had so thankfully found in the bed of the truck.

"Don't worry about him," he assured her as he stepped away, "I can handle him." He peeked through a few of the windows — all clear, for now. "Probably be a lot more of them as soon as they find out about us." He circled back around, past the girl, checking things out, collecting information about his surroundings. Now that he was over his initial shock from this appalling night, he was back on top of his game.

Which brought him around to the next order of business. "The truck is out of gas," he explained, then gestured toward the side of the house with the tire iron. "This pump out here is locked. Is there a key?"

Nothing from the blonde. Just that stricken, child-like gaze.

Despite his initial relief at finding her, his frustration grew. "We can try to get out of here if we can get some gas. Is there a *key*?"

Still nothing.

Great. He turned from her to hide and control his irritation — Lord only knew what she had already been through herself tonight! — and his eyes laid upon a telephone. He knelt before it and dialed the operator, but got nothing.

Movement behind him, but it was just the blonde. "I suppose you've tried this," he commented, more to himself than to her. He hung up, collected the tire iron, and followed after her into the hallway.

"Do you live here?" he asked. By now his guess was that she didn't, but he was still hoping for *some* kind of useful information from her.

But this time she didn't even look at him. She was gazing up the stairs, her hand trembling before her face, her complexion pale and sallow. She began to quietly sob.

Ben peered up the stairs and saw that the girl had not been just staring blankly, but looking at something specific up on the landing. Gripping his tire iron, he climbed the stairs to investigate.

Before he reached the top, he found his breath drifting away. He had to pull himself up the bannister, hand over hand, to make it as far as he did. He gaped at the corpse with the eaten face as it stared back at him.

"Jesus ..." he whispered. After everything he had seen at Beekman's Diner, he thought he had passed his shock threshold, though that nausea and disgust had been shoved aside by survival instincts. But in spite of what he'd witnessed with the janitor, old man Joe, and the others ... this masticated corpse still got to him in a way for which he was not prepared.

Rushing back down the stairs, he braced himself in the corner of the hallway for a moment, fighting to control both his gag reflex and his sanity. The girl remained slumped against the wall, clutching the kitchen knife to her chest and rocking gently side to side, staring into nothingness; if she had any reaction to Ben's momentary breakdown, she gave no sign.

"We've gotta get out of here," Ben said when he could trust himself to speak. "We have to get to where there's some other people." He touched her arm, trying to reassure her, before moving away.

Barbra stared after the man in the sweater as he disappeared down the hallway. Her thoughts were still muddy, but she knew she did *not* want to be alone anymore. She wanted to tell her new companion something about Johnny, but for the moment, she could not remember *what* it was about her brother that she needed to share.

Following after the man with slow, unsteady steps, she

heard him saying from the kitchen, "We'd better take some food. I'll see if I can find some food ..."

As Barbra inched her way down the hallway, she struggled to regain some equilibrium. She ran her hands along a sideboard, along the wall of the stairs. Real things, *normal* things, everyday things that had nothing to do with vicious creatures lurking through her father's cemetery, wandering around outside the house ...

A dripping sound drew her attention. She looked around, unable to locate the source. Was it coming from the kitchen? Had the man turned on the tap and left it ... but no, the sound was closer than that. It was here, in the hallway.

She looked down, then up. It was blood, dripping down in slow, syrupy strings from the body on the second-floor and collecting in a thick puddle very near her feet. Even as she noticed, some of it dripped onto her hand.

Biting against a yelp, Barbra pushed away from the wall, rushing into the living room and brushing the gooey, half-dried blood from her hand onto her coat. It was repulsive, but still ... the jolt served to snap her out of her fugue, if just a little, and for that (as sick as it sounded) she was grateful. Feeling a little more like herself again, she followed the man into the kitchen.

He was going through the drawers and the refrigerator, making more of a racket than she would have preferred. The sharp noise jabbed at her ears, triggering some of the haze to return, and she struggled to hold on to her focus, partial though it was. She noticed that the man had left his tire iron on top of the refrigerator and she picked it up — he glanced up and saw her doing so, but did not seem to mind. The iron was solid, comforting; in some ways, it made her feel better than her own knife.

Holding both weapons in her hands, she asked the

man, "What's happening?"

The man glanced at her again, then mumbled, "What the hell do you think is happening?" as he returned to digging through the refrigerator.

"What's *happening*?" she repeated, this time with more force, and she did not like the shrill quality of her own voice.

This time the man paid more attention to her. He rested the bag he'd been using to gather supplies on top of the refrigerator and leaned forward, a heavy sigh escaping as he did so. His expression was very earnest as he opened his mouth to say something, hopefully to answer her, but the sound of breaking glass captured both of their attention.

For a moment, Barbra's heart seized in panic. The windows! Were they breaking through the *windows*?!

But no, the sound was coming from outside somewhere. Thank God.

Ben, having the same initial reaction, had retrieved his tire iron from the girl, but then he drew the same conclusion. Unfortunately, unlike her, he had a bad idea what the sound might actually be. He rushed into the next room to look out the window toward the front of the house.

He was right and wrong. The sound of breaking glass had indeed come from the truck, but it was not the windshield or side windows being broken as he had feared. It seemed the things outside were smashing at the headlights, which he had left on in his rush to get the girl into the house.

Those things don't like the bright light, he thought. *Too much like fire?*

Then he belatedly absorbed his own use of the plural.

"Two of them," he muttered aloud. He glanced back and forth between the assaulted truck and the blonde woman. She seemed more lucid than before — at least she was now speaking to him.

Taking her by the shoulders, he told her, emphatically, "There are *two* of them out there. Have you seen any more around here?"

"I ..."

"I can take care of those two."

"I ... don't know ..."

"I know you're afraid but we have—"

The girl erupted, "I - *don't* - KNOOOW!" She thrashed about, struggling under his hands without actually trying to break away. What concerned Ben the most was the large knife she was still holding, and as she repeated, "I - *don't* - know!" he lowered his grip to pin her arms, and the next thing he knew, he had shoved her back into an armchair with far more force than intended. But the knife fell away and she burst into tears, blubbering "What's happening?!" and sobbing.

Fine. He would have to act now with what information he had.

Gritting his teeth in anticipation, Ben opened the front door and stepped out into the night.

He reached the edge of the porch just as the second headlight was shattered, plunging him into near-darkness. He lifted the tire iron, ready to strike at a moment's notice. Studying the two, he could make out enough detail to see that neither of these were the one he'd spotted upon first reaching the house and pushing the girl inside — these were two new ones, which meant he was alone out here with at least *three*, maybe more.

He also noticed that these two were a little different from the others he had seen up close since this all started. The nurse, the patient ... most of them had been visibly injured, while others had appeared normal if not for their violent behavior and impaired movement.

But these two, they fell into neither category. They were both disheveled, but did not appear injured. And they *stank*, terribly — they reeked of decay, like road kill left in the sun. And as they spotted and approached him, he could make out the distress of their skin, the look of decomposing, necrotizing tissue.

Good God, could any communicable disease cause such rapid degradation? Maybe it wasn't a disease at all, but something else — a toxic gas perhaps, or even some sort of chemical exposure? *None* of these possibilities brought Ben any comfort, but as he approached the nearest one, the tire iron held at ready, he fought against the disgust of getting any closer to these things; he would do what had to be done, to protect himself and the girl.

The first one just stood there as Ben swung the tire iron around to smash him in the side of the neck. With the mildest of grunts, the man dropped to the ground, but was still moving — knowing how difficult these things were to put down, Ben moved in for the kill. Again and again, he struck the man as he — *it* — struggled to get up again. He hit it in the face, neck, shoulder, over and over.

Why wouldn't they just stop? What kept them going?

The first one was *finally* lying still, but then grasping hands tugged at him, and Ben realized that the other one was upon him. He shoved it away, hard enough to knock its clumsy feet out from under it, and then he was doing it again — crouched over the fetid thing, hitting it over and over; each blow should have been enough to knock it out, or at least send it into a stupor.

But it kept moving, kept trying to get up, kept clawing at him. So Ben hit it.

Again and again ...

Back in the house, Barbra remained where the man in the sweater had pushed her — in a distant way, she understood that her new companion was just trying to help her, to help both of them, but she was lost, so lost. Her sense of time, her feeling of reality, were detaching again.

Wild thoughts tumbled through her mind ...

... of savage creatures and cemeteries ...

... of puddles of blood ...

... of Johnny fussing with his driving gloves ...

She wanted to get a grip on herself, she really did, but she couldn't remember how.

And so she remained oblivious as the back door into the kitchen was forced open, as a mutilated man with a ripped-open throat shambled into the house, as he shuffled his way forward until his glassy eyes managed to focus on Barbra collapsed in the chair, and as his course found direction, toward her ...

Panting, Ben realized that the second one had finally stopped moving, too. Feeling drained and sore, his body already aching from exertion and prolonged tension, he pushed himself to his feet. He leaned against a tree to recuperate, splitting his focus between the two bodies and the surrounding area. The very first one still had not wandered back into view, but Ben had no doubts that it was out there, somewhere in the darkness. He had kept his struggle with these two as quiet as possible, but he couldn't depend on that having worked.

Forcing himself to pick up the pace, he climbed the porch and stepped into the house, pulling the screen door closed behind—

Ben saw the thing with the torn up throat and bloody shirt in the kitchen, approaching the girl where she still sat, clueless and rubbing at her face, in the chair.

Rushing forward, he reached out to pull the girl from harm's way. She looked startled and confused at first, but soon followed his gaze toward this newest danger, and did not resist. The thing entered the living room and was reaching out to them, but unlike most of the others, who had only clawed at Ben in hunger or anger or whatever the hell motivated them, this one looked almost beseeching as its hand waved through the air between them.

Ben pushed the girl behind him, and then she did one of the first useful things he had seen her do: She crossed the room and closed and locked the front door which he had left standing open.

Thank God, he thought, grateful for some real help. But that was as far as he got before the thing was on him, moaning and gasping through its mangled throat.

Ben swung in with the tire iron, but this time he missed his mark. The thing's entreating hand blocked his arm, and the tire iron fell to the floor. He immediately tried to retrieve it, but the thing was grabbing at his sweater, its teeth bared, moaning with more vehemence. Attempts to tug his arms free got him nowhere, so he pivoted around, taking the thing with him in a twisted mockery of a slow dance, then shoved it forward and followed it down to the floor.

His plan only partly worked. He succeeded in pinning it to the floor, himself on top and mostly in control, but their shared momentum had not carried them as far as he had hoped — the tire iron remained barely out of his reach.

The thing gasped and gurgled louder still, raking fingers at his eyes, teeth gnashing as it tried to bite him anywhere it could manage. Its pale face and curdled wound sickened him, and he found the burst of energy needed to knock its arms away long enough to seize his weapon.

Raising the tire iron high, Ben drove it down with both arms, the tapered end of the tool boring straight through the thing's forehead. Unlike those he had put down before it, this one stopped struggling immediately, its limbs falling limp like a puppet with its strings cut.

Still, Ben almost panicked when the iron would not come free at first, and he pulled harder, tugging with his whole upper body as he sought proper leverage. He needed his weapon back, could not relax for an instant unless he was armed. For all he knew the thing was just stunned, would start moving again at any moment, like all those others who refused to go quietly—

The tire iron came free, the thing's head plopping back to the floor with finality, a murky fluid oozing from the hole in its forehead, unsettling in both its runny consistency and its lack of volume.

Ben stumbled away from it, holding his dripping weapon before him, unsure of how to clean away the substance that was so little like blood. He slumped against the door into the kitchen, his knees trembling and his breathing quick and shallow. For a moment, he envied the girl's recourse, to just shut down and push every aspect of this Godforsaken night away.

Then he glanced through the open door leading onto the back porch, and saw no reprieve — another one was coming, a man dressed in his pajamas and robe, looking like nothing more than an everyday working man ready for bed; were it not for his familiar, unsteady movement, Ben might have thought he was a neighbor seeking refuge.

Shoving away from the wall while he still had adrenaline left to move him, Ben rushed the robed man and slammed the tire iron right between his eyes. This one reacted more normally than most of them, clutching his hands to his ruined face as he stumbled away — Ben might have feared that he had made a mistake, except that the man made no sound. And then Ben saw that this was the least of his worries.

The robed man was not alone. There were half a dozen of them in the backyard, all in various states of dress (or undress) and dishevelment. But they all moved the same way, all had that empty, soulless expression on their faces, in their eyes.

Too many, too many of them for him to fight alone. Ben closed and locked the door ...

... and as soon as it was sealed, his knees threatened to buckle from underneath him. Leaning heavily against the door, he forced himself to take slow, even breaths.

"They know we're in here now ..."

In the next room, Barbra barely heard him. She was focused on the creature on the floor, the one which had crept up behind her through the kitchen, the one with the torn throat ... the one which now had a hole in his forehead.

Her movements slow, her awareness fuzzy and trance-like, Barbra crept toward the creature.

Are ... are its eyes still moving?

Surely not. Whatever had taken possession of these people, whatever had driven them to such awful mania and murderous behavior, surely a shaft of metal driven *into its head* was enough to finally kill it for good.

Closer still she crept, mesmerized.

Its eyes *were* moving. Its eyes, but nothing else — its arms and legs remained loose on the floor, its jaw relaxed, its teeth no longer bared and snarling. But its eyes danced around, back and forth, until they finally laid upon her, that hollow look with its parody of life locked onto her, the need still evident even with no other means of expressing it.

Barbra stared. And stared. Leaning forward, ready to take another step, almost close enough to touch it—

"Don't look at it!"

The words startled her, and the creature was dragged

away by the man in the sweater.

Ben was unnerved to find the girl staring so intently at the thing's face. He, too, saw that its eyes had locked onto her. He would have expected anyone to feel the same revulsion as he, but despite how rattled and disjointed she had been since he'd come upon her on the front porch of the house, the girl now seemed almost spellbound by the thing. And whatever these people were turning into, Ben was pretty damned sure they weren't vampires.

They're not ... *right?*

Don't even go there. Until one of them shows up shouting, "Come out, Neville!", just put that thought right out of your fool head.

He didn't mean to snap at the girl when he told her not to look at it, but her behavior scared him. He grabbed the thing by the ankles and dragged it into the kitchen, toward the back door.

The last thing he wanted to do was to open it, to go back out there with *them*, but he couldn't have this one in the house with its roving eyes, and he didn't quite have the stomach to smash into its head again while it was just lying there.

Opening the door and peering outside, Ben found the group of them just standing there, staring at the house, but as soon as they saw him, they began moving forward again. Still, they were far enough away that he could dispose of it, if he hurried.

If only he could *keep* them away from the house, long enough for him and the girl to ...

A keen idea presented itself. Keen and *disturbing*, but he was being granted precious few compromises tonight. He would have to set aside his qualms and do what needed to be done.

So many discarded scruples, so much weight on my

conscience in such a short time. If I live to see the light of dawn, how much of me will remain?

Ben dragged the body with its moving eyes and torn throat out through the door and to the very edge of the back porch. He considered the dangers of what he had in mind, and knew that it might be safer to pull it further out into the yard. But the others were closing in, so he'd take his chances with the lesser evil.

Squatting beside the body, he reached into his pocket and pulled out his book of matches.

Casting about with a weary eye, he struck the match and touched it to where the body's clothes were loosest — its untucked shirt, an inverted pants pocket, along the cuff of its sleeve ...

The others were drawing closer. He was almost out of time.

When the flame finally took in earnest, he was caught off guard by its sudden intensity — one moment he feared that the clothes might not catch well enough, the next he nearly lost his eyebrows. He stood and kicked the body off the porch into the grass, grateful that it rolled far enough away that the flames weren't licking at the wooden steps.

And just as he had hoped, the others held warding hands and arms before their faces and retreated — not far, but he would take what he could get. Just as he had seen at Beekman's, they might not have much else going on upstairs, but they did not like fire.

Then the smoke — and the stomach-churning stench — forced Ben to retreat himself. He returned to the house, shut and locked the back door. Then for good measure, he grabbed the small breakfast table and shoved it up against the door.

As before, he allowed himself the luxury of a brief respite, leaning against the little table and wiping the sweat from his brow.

The girl stared at him from the kitchen doorway, saying nothing. If she had seen what he'd just done, she gave no indication, passed no judgement one way or the other.

Then Ben's gaze fell upon something across the kitchen, and he realized what they had to do next — the only thing they could do, until some kind of help arrived.

Moving across the room, he opened the toolbox and tried rooting around, but he couldn't see a damn thing in the dark. Then again, as he had pointed out before, their presence was no longer a secret, so why hinder their efforts further?

Flicking on the kitchen light, he dove back into the toolbox as he told the girl, "Get some more lights on in this house."

The girl appeared dazed by the sudden illumination, but she tottered around without comment and headed back into the next room, presumably to follow his suggestion.

That wasn't a suggestion, Ben. You just gave her an order.

Fine. He had given her an order — so be it. He had always known when to put his foot down, and until she snapped out of her daze, now was the time.

So Ben collected tools: A screwdriver from this toolbox; a hammer from the box next to it; then he rooted through drawers and found what he really wanted — *nails*, lots of nails.

Gathering them in his hands, he glanced up and saw the girl had returned, her knife again within close reach on top of the refrigerator. He had no idea how long she'd been back, or if she had followed his suggestion (his order) to turn on more lights. So he tried a different tact.

"Why don't you see if you can find some wood," he

told her as he worked, "some boards, something there by the fireplace. Something so we can nail this place up."

But when he looked up again, all she had done was wander further into the kitchen, still looking at him with that lost, confused expression on her face, asking him without words to take care of her, to make it all better.

Throwing down the tools, he snapped, "Look, goddamn it—!" before catching himself. No excuse — he might have decided to take charge, but she wasn't a *soldier*, either.

Taking a cooling breath, he walked over to her and took her by the shoulders again, gently this time. "Look ... I know you're afraid. I'm afraid, too. But we have to try to board the house up *together*. Now I'm going to board up the windows and the doors. Do you understand?"

Still that blank stare, but at least she appeared to be listening.

"We'll be all right here," he continued, slow and emphatic. "We'll be all right here until someone comes to rescue us. But we'll have to work *together*. You'll have to *help* me. Now I want you to go and get some wood so I can board the place up. Do you understand? Okay? *Okay?*"

On the second "okay," she finally, and thankfully, responded with a nod. It was a little unfocused, her head bobbing a little too loose on her neck, but at least it suggested that she was absorbing what he said to her. She turned around on her own, and Ben gave her a slight, soft push as she again left the kitchen. Sighing, he returned to his scavenger hunt.

Shuffling her feet, Barbra soon found herself back in the study. Not as dark now with a few more lights on, she found the mounted animal heads less intimidating. She stood for a moment, looking around, trying to remember why she had come in here ... and then the mantle over the fireplace brought it back to her. Yes, she had seen the fireplace earlier, and the man in the sweater had told her to ... to gather wood, yes.

He was a nice man, really. She didn't mind that he was a little harsh at times. She had known far harsher men, like her grandfather. Why, if she and Johnny ...

Johnny ... something about Johnny sent a chill up her spine, and she pushed it away. Where was Johnny right now, anyway? And ... why had she come in here again?

Confused though she was, Barbra was not completely out of touch. She knew that danger lurked outside, she knew that something was terribly, terribly wrong with these people, these creatures, even though she did not understand *what* was wrong.

Perhaps she should pray. Yes, that's what her grandfather would have told her. Pray to God for forgiveness of her sins, for deliverance from this punishment for ... for ...

For what? What could she possibly have done to deserve *this* night? Even Johnny, who hadn't been to church for a while, didn't deserve—

Her hand, which had been absently trailing along a table, dragged across a doily and onto a music box. Striking the button atop, it opened little doors and began turning as its sweet, tinny melody played away.

Far from startling her, it took Barbra a moment to realize that she was hearing it at all. She had been thinking about Johnny ... something about her poor brother Johnny...

Round and round the music box turned as Barbra stared at it. Round and round, round and round ...

In the kitchen, Ben had just finished removing one of the inner house doors from its hinges. Rather than just nailing random wood across the entrances, he figured the weight of the door would serve as a greater barricade. He added the ironing board to his pile, and then noticed that the bottom shelves of one of the cabinets had been crudely boarded up at some point. He grabbed hold of the plank and tugged until, with a screech of dragging nails, it ripped free, revealing something of a jackpot — more planks of wood, stored within along with other odds and ends; the owners must've done most of their own handiwork. He gathered all of it up and dumped it into his growing lumber pile.

The increasing noise finally jolted Barbra from her reverie. She looked around, becoming aware of her surroundings once more, and her gaze fell upon the fireplace. Yes, *that* was why she was in here — not for the music box, but for the fireplace. Wood. She was supposed to gather wood.

Crouching before the fireplace, she gathered a small pile in her arms. She then stood, looked back at the music box and around the room, and — determined to prove herself of some use — returned to the kitchen where the man in the sweater was making so much racket.

He was hefting a door upright — where in the world had he found a loose door? — as she walked in. He glanced at her, then carried the door over to the outer wall, placing it longways across the back entrance. Why was he—?

Then Barbra figured out what he had in mind. Slowly, the wheels in her head were starting to turn again; she wished she were recovering faster, but didn't know what to do about it. She placed her rather pathetic pile of wood atop the refrigerator and shuffled across the room to help him.

He had his hammer and nails ready, so Barbra reached out to steady the makeshift barricade for him. He again glanced at her, this time offering a slight, reassuring smile, then he began to pound nails.

The sharp noise was an instant bane to Barbra, driving through her ears and even, it felt, through her eyes into her brain. She wanted to help, she tried moving around him as he worked back and forth, tried to brace the door for him wherever she could while he hammered. But that noise! It unsettled her more than it should have, reminded her too much of the rock slamming into the car window as the creature from the cemetery tried to get to her.

Before long, she was just standing there again — feeble, useless.

Thankfully, the man finished his work in short order. He tugged at the barricade a few times, his demeanor satisfied. He muttered, "That'll hold," then turned and said directly to her, "They're not that strong." He picked up a little plastic box from the kitchen counter and pushed it into her hands. She looked down and saw that it was filled with nails and screws, thumbtacks and paperclips. "I want you to find some nails," he told her, "pick out the biggest ones you can find."

Then off he went, on the move. Barbra followed, determined to help.

Time blurred somewhat as Ben lost himself in the work. He focused on the simple tasks, boarding, nailing, hammering, not allowing himself to dwell on recent events. If he thought about those details, he might start to wallow in it, and he didn't have that luxury. His hands started to feel the burn, the early warning of blisters to come, but he didn't care — better to grow some calluses doing this than ... other things.

The girl remained quiet, but she followed along with him and pitched in when he needed it. He could tell that the noise bothered her, but she voiced no complaint. As they ran low on stopgap lumber, he decided to try and coax her further out of her shell.

"Yeah, this room looks pretty secure," he commented as he leaned through the next doorway and turned on the lights. "If we have to, we can run in here and board up the doors."

A trickle down the back of his neck revealed that he was perspiring from his efforts, something he'd failed to notice until now. As he spoke, he stripped his sweater from his white dress shirt and gathered their meager supply of wood. "Won't be long before those things come back, pounding their way in here, but they're *afraid* now."

As he moved into the living room, he looked around and realized just where to get more wood. Setting his armload to one side, he began rolling up his sleeves.

"They're afraid of fire. I found *that* out."

Pushing chairs away from the modest dining table, he rolled the table cloth around the centerpiece and removed the whole bundle, setting it to one side.

"You know a place back down the road called Beekman's ...?"

As Ben upended the dining table and used a hammer to remove the legs, he told the girl about his experiences at the diner, the events which, for him, started this God-awful night. He left out many of the details, didn't bother to share the demise of the old man or the janitor, but he did tell her about the gasoline truck, about the things' reaction to the fire, the way they stared at him, and how *he* reacted by running them over. And though it brought up some of the very thoughts he wanted to avoid, he had hoped to find the sharing at least somewhat *cathartic* ... but instead, it just upset him more and more as he spoke. He finally had to turn away and regain control of himself.

But his tale did accomplish one thing — Barbra

listened to him.

Barbra had folded the tablecloth and, as she found her way to a nearby chair, sat with it in her lap, listening. She liked his voice, which could be as gentle as it was forceful. And his tone, the emotions therein, like a sincere confession to clergy, prompted her to want to share as well.

So Barbra began telling her own story, of her and Johnny's trip to the cemetery.

Ben was glad that the girl was talking again, but she didn't seem to realize how disjointed her own narrative came across. She spoke of Johnny, which Ben soon deduced was her brother, and then began complaining of the heat and tugged at her coat without actually removing it. As Ben muscled the dining tabletop over to the nearby windows, the girl's story continued to build — whereas his sharing had drained him, hers was working her up. By the time she got to the part where a man approached them in the cemetery, Ben finally caught her name — *Barbra* — but he did not care for the sharp edge in her voice.

Fearing hysterics, he suggested, "Why don't you just ... keep calm?"

But the girl was on a roll now. She described the man's attack, and the very hysterics Ben had dreaded threatened to overtake her.

"I think you should just *calm down*," he repeated, putting more steel into his voice.

As she reached the climax of her story, the part where her brother fought her attacker (and Ben could guess how that struggle probably ended), she did lose some steam, but only to turn in another direction.

"We've got ... we have to wait for Johnny," she said.

Ben avoided eye contact as he bustled around the room. What was there to say? He had hoped that getting her talking would help focus her, but now he doubted that it was a good idea after all. Because if she went where he next expected—

"We ... we'd better go out and get him."

Ben swallowed a sigh. Sure enough, there it was. Her talkative shift was misleading—she still didn't *understand* what her own story meant.

"We have to go out and get Johnny," she insisted.

Not sure what else to do, Ben made a big show of how busy he was and ignored her. He moved the ironing board toward the front door of the house.

"He's out there," Barbra continued, her voice getting shrill now. "*Please*, don't you hear me? We've got to go out and get him. Please! *We have got to go get Johnny*!"

Then she was on her feet, following him. He glanced at her, at the pain and dread on her now-livid face. He saw that, somewhere deep inside, she knew the truth. Then he looked away.

But Barbra wasn't having it. "*Please, help me!*" She grabbed him by the arm, yanking him back around with surprising force. "*PLEASE!*"

"Don't you know what's going on out there?" he demanded, his frustration getting the better of him. "This is no Sunday school picnic—"

She threw herself at him; he caught her arms before she grabbed at him again. "Don't you understand? My brother is *alone*!"

As gently as he could, Ben told her, "Your brother is *dead*."

"*NO!*" Barbra ripped her arms free. "My brother is *not* dead!"

And with that, she bolted for the front door.

Ben caught her before she could open it, lifting her whole body in his arms and pulling her away.

She struggled free with an offended grunt, stared death

at him for about two seconds, then slapped him across the face.

Ben took the slap, glared back for about the same amount of time, then hauled off and returned what she had given him, with interest.

Barbra moaned and looked up at him in surprise ... then her eyes rolled back in her head and she collapsed. For the barest moment, Ben considered letting her hit the floor, but then his better nature got the best of him and he caught her in his arms. He carried her to the sofa, setting her down with care. He took a few steps back, then bent over again to open her coat for her.

Should he do more? He wasn't sure, but he didn't have the luxury of pampering her right now. Part of him felt guilty for it but the fact was, he was relieved that she would be out of his hair for the time being.

Leaving her there on the sofa, he returned to boarding up the house ...

Time blurred again for Ben, especially without his having to keep a furtive eye on the girl — on Barbra. He moved from window to window, bracing, hammering, testing, hammering some more. The mundane activity crept over his nerves, soothing them, but at the same time it almost whispered that *surely* what he had experienced this night had been nothing more than his imagination. Perhaps a hallucination, brought on by eating a spoiled hamburger at Beekman's Diner — there was more of gravy than of grave about those things! They *couldn't* be real. Could they?

But for better or worse, he was too practical to give in to that sweet temptation.

As he was finishing up the living room windows, he noticed for the first time an old-style radio through the study doorway. He hadn't seen one like this in quite a while, and his enthusiasm was tempered with concern that it might no longer work. Still, he had to try — anything to gain more information, *any* information, about what was happening.

Kneeling before the oversized, wooden-shelled device, he turned it on, and sure enough, it remained silent for several long seconds. He was ready to give up when he finally heard a whine and some static, and adjusted the controls — after a few more false starts, he found a clear signal.

"Because of the obvious threat to untold numbers of citizens," came the announcer's voice, which sounded uncharacteristically tense by professional standards, *"and because of the crisis which is even now developing, this radio station will remain on the air, day and night."*

Breathing a sigh of relief, Ben listened.

"This station, and hundreds of other radio and TV stations throughout this part of the country, are pooling their resources through an emergency network hookup, to keep you informed of all developments."

Deciding that stagnation was not the best idea, Ben stood and returned to his work. As the announcer continued, he hammered away in a few more places, still listening.

"At this hour, we repeat, these are the facts as we know them: There is an epidemic of mass-murder, being committed by a virtual army of unidentified assassins."

"Assassins," Ben mused. *That makes it sound so ... clean.* Then he rebuked his own reaction. *"Clean," Ben? Dear God. How's that for a sad state of affairs!*

He continued to hammer, and continued to listen.

"The murders are taking place in villages, cities, rural homes, and suburbs — with no apparent pattern or reason for the slayings. It seems to be a sudden, general

explosion of mass homicide.

"We have some descriptions of the assassins: Eyewitnesses say they are 'ordinary-looking' people; some say they appear to be in a kind of trance. *Others describe them as being ..."*

The voice faded away from Ben for a moment as he took a look outside through one of the unboarded windows.

There were now three— no, *four* of the things in the front yard, most of them hovering around the truck. With the headlights knocked out, they were no longer attacking the vehicle, but still ... if he could find the keys to the gas pump, the truck was their best ticket to escape — if the barricades failed them, they would have to run.

So how could he keep them away from the truck?

Use what you know. If it's not broken, don't fix it.

Thinking, Ben moved into the study as the radio played on.

"... so, at this point, there is no really authentic way for us to say who or what to look for, and guard yourself against. Misshapen 'monsters' ..."

Ben found lighter fluid on the mantle, but the floor around the fireplace was bare from when Barbra collected the wood. Where would they keep ...?

Ah! He opened the adjoining closet, and there it was — beneath the hanging coats, a small box of chopped wood and kindling. He dragged the box out and deposited it in front of the fireplace.

"Reaction of law-enforcement officials is one of complete bewilderment at this hour. So far, we have been unable to determine if any kind of organized investigation is yet underway."

Tossing several logs into the fireplace, Ben dowsed them with the lighter fluid.

"Police, sheriff deputies, and emergency ambulances are literally deafened with calls for help. The scene can best be described as mayhem."

Ben got the fire started, then collected the lighter fluid and returned to the living room. He grabbed a large armchair and dragged it over toward the front door.

"Mayors of Pittsburgh, Philadelphia, and Miami, along with the governors of several Eastern and Midwestern states, have indicated the National Guard may be mobilized at any moment, but that has not happened as yet."

Ben dowsed the chair with lighter fluid, shaking the fluid over it and then finally squeezing the can into a stronger stream, thoroughly soaking the seat cushion and arms of the chair to the point that the fumes made him a little lightheaded.

"The only advice our reporters have been able to get from official sources is for private citizens to stay in their homes, behind locked doors. Do not venture outside for any reason, until the nature of this crisis has been determined, and until we can advise what course of action to take."

Moving to a window, Ben jerked one of the curtains free from the rod, then knelt on the floor and tore off a sizeable strip of fabric. He had never actually tried this sort of thing before, but he had seen it done in the movies and was confident it would work.

"Keep listening to radio and TV for any special instructions as this crisis develops further."

Ben wrapped the torn cloth around the thicker end of one of the remaining dining table legs, twisting the cloth tight as he carried it back into the study.

"Thousands of office and factory workers are being urged to stay at their places of employment, not *to make*

any attempt to get to their homes."

Thrusting the wrapped end of the table leg into the fireplace, Ben was encouraged to see the fabric catch fire in an instant. But when he withdrew his makeshift torch, he was startled by how much noxious smoke billowed from it.

Holding the torch away from his face, he headed back toward the front door.

"*However, in spite of this urging and warning, streets and highways are packed with frantic people trying to reach their families, or attempting to flee just* anywhere."

Knocking aside lumber that blocked his way, Ben unlocked the front door, then took stock: Was he ready for this? Was everything set?

"*We repeat: The safest course of action at this time is simply to stay where you are.*"

Easy for you to say, buddy!

Opening the front door, Ben pushed the chair outside ahead of him, not stopping until he reached the end of the porch.

The things — maybe five or six of them now — immediately focused from wherever they were gazing to the house, to him. Where the hell were they coming from? They didn't speak, barely made any noise at all, so how the hell was "word" spreading to come here?

He had no answers, and suspected that none would be forthcoming. The important thing was to keep them away from the house until he could finish barricading it, and, if at all possible, away from the truck.

Ben touched the torch to the chair, and it went up like a bonfire! One or two of the things actually moaned in apprehension, fire once more wringing more emotion from them than anything else. He kicked the chair hard, sending it toppling over into the front yard, eliciting more groans from the things as they backed away.

He tossed the torch toward them for good measure, stepping back into the doorway as he watched them. As he had hoped, their retreat carried them away from the truck — they no longer acknowledged anything save the fire before them. With luck, the chair would burn and smolder for a while to come.

Withdrawing into the house, he closed and locked the door.

"Ladies and gentlemen, we've just received word that the President has called a meeting of his Cabinet to deal with the sudden epidemic of murder which has seized the eastern third of this nation. The meeting is scheduled to convene within the hour."

Wanting to capitalize on the extra breathing room he had just bought, Ben wasted no time in collecting another plank of wood and hurrying to the window he had stripped of a curtain. Balancing the lumber with his elbow, he was back to hammering, hammering ...

"Members of the Presidential Cabinet will be joined by officials of the FBI and ..."

Hammering and nailing, boarding and hammering, soon completing this room — as well as sporting sore arms and blistered hands. He had considered moving the piano over to block the front door but it wasn't on rollers, and decided it would be more effort than it was worth. All the while he worked, he kept an ear open to the radio as the news droned on, often looping back around and repeating very little new, and almost nothing truly useful.

"... behind closed doors. The White House spokesman, in announcing this conference, says there will be an official announcement as soon as possible, following that meeting. This is the latest dispatch, just received in our news room."

Down to little more for lumber than a single removed door, Ben prepared to head into the next room. He glanced over to check on Barbra, but she had barely moved. He knew that he had not hit her that hard, that this was more of a faint than anything else, but could he blame her? Better to let her sleep it off as long as possible.

"Latest word also from national press services in Washington D.C. now tells us that the emergency Presidential conference, which we've just mentioned, will include high-ranking scientists from the National Aeronautics and Space Administration ..."

He carried the lumber into the hallway by the staircase, which took him past another door that he could remove from its hinges. He touched it, swiveling it to and fro, feeling its weight. He would come back to it later, when Barbra was awake and less likely to be disturbed by the noise. He was glad to have noticed it, though, as this reminded him to go around and remove other doors from other rooms in the house.

What Ben did *not* notice, however, was the nondescript, smaller door directly behind it, leading into the wall. A door which opened into this very room where Barbra slept, helpless ...

Finding a different door further from where Barbra lay, Ben began hammering his screwdriver into the hinges. This one refused to give easily, and it was tedious work. He couldn't really hear the radio from here, but he was losing faith as to how useful it was proving, anyway. He had to keep moving, because he wasn't sure how much longer he could keep up this pace ...

Barbra gradually became aware of a man's voice, unfamiliar and tinny. It took her a moment to remember where she was, she was so groggy.

"... have joined their facilities in an emergency

network, to bring you this news as it develops."

Her cheek hurt. Why did her cheek hurt? She lifted a hand to probe along her jaw with gentle fingers.

"*We urge you to stay tuned to radio and TV, and to stay indoors at all costs.*"

It all came back to her — most of it, anyway. The cemetery, Johnny's teasing her, a man who was really a creature chasing her to this house. She remembered now that the man in the sweater, who saved her from the thing with the torn throat, had struck her, but — to her embarrassment — she recalled that she had slapped him first. Why had she done that? Something about Johnny, she thought.

"*Late reports reaching this newsroom tell of frightened people seeking refuge in churches, schools, and government buildings, demanding shelter and protection from the wholesale murder, which apparently is engulfing much of the nation.*"

Sitting up, Barbra strove for the focus which had eluded her for some time now. She heard banging somewhere else in the house, but ... yes, she remembered, that would be her companion boarding up the house, a task she had promised herself she would help with but had so far failed.

She would help him, she would. She just needed a moment to get her bearings ...

In the other room, Ben finished covering one of the larger windows. Satisfied, he turned to step down from the couch he had used as a stepladder ... and he stumbled. His head seemed to keep turning even after his neck had stopped, and he had to lean back against the wall to avoid falling over.

Okay, that's it. Time for a break, tough guy.

Yes, it was.

Flopping down onto the couch, he let the hammer fall free and drew a deep breath. He hadn't taken a moment to truly rest since everything went to hell at Beekman's, and he wasn't going to do himself or Barbra any good if he passed out from exhaustion.

Exhaling, he glanced over to the left breast pocket of his shirt and barely hesitated before fishing for his pack of cigarettes. He had been trying to quit or at least cut back, to serve as a better role-model for his impressionable students, and his efforts must have been working because he had not even thought about having a smoke since all of this started.

Which was kind of funny, because in that moment of quietus, he had never needed a cigarette more in his whole life.

Lighting up, he sucked the nicotine deep into his lungs, luxuriating in the familiar burn. Now that he was still, he could make out a few snippets from the radio, but it didn't amount to much more than he already knew — telling people to get off the streets, to go home and lock their doors, et cetera, et cetera.

Glancing around the room, he noticed yet another door he could unhinge and use — one thing was for sure, this house was providing no shortage of improvised lumber. This door didn't connect room-to-room, but appeared to be another closet. He sat a second longer, determined to take his much-needed break and enjoy his first cigarette since Friday ... but in the next moment he was climbing to his feet.

Opening the closet, he perused it for anything useful. It was filled with coats, jackets, and other winter gear, and God knew it was hot enough in the house as it was. Maybe he could tear some of them into strips, in case he needed another torch?

Then he glanced down to the floor and noticed several pairs of women's shoes.

Kneeling down, he thought about Barbra in the other room, thought about her stockinged feet. Reaching into the closet, he bypassed the high-heels for a pair of sensible flats — with any luck, they might fit her well enough.

Standing, he took one last look in the closet for anything else of value ... and a moment later, he thanked God Almighty that he had made the extra effort.

A rifle!

Excited, he seized the weapon — a *real* weapon! — and pulled it out. It was an older hunting rifle, but it felt like salvation in his hands.

Setting his cigarette aside, he dug through the closet in earnest, knocking aside shoes, then feeling around the top shelf, searching, searching ...

He laid his hand upon a shoebox tucked out of sight at the back of the shelf, a shoebox with the weight he was hoping for — too heavy for shoes.

A satisfied grin flickered across his face as he pulled the shoebox down. Placing it on the floor, he tossed the lid aside.

Ammunition. And lots of it.

Yes!

Replacing the lid and tucking the box under his arm, feeling a sense of confidence for the first time in hours, Ben kicked the closet door shut and headed back into the living room.

He was mildly surprised to find Barbra sitting upright; she was shrugging out of her coat, but she stopped when he entered the room. He knelt down in front of her, but she just stared off into space — he had no idea if she remembered their tussle, or if she was even fully aware of his presence; if the droning of danger from the radio had affected her either way, it did not show.

"I found a gun and some bullets out there," he told her. "Oh, and these."

He held the shoes up for her inspection, but she didn't so much as glance at them, just kept staring straight ahead. Shrugging to himself, he proceeded to put the shoes on her feet for her.

"This place is boarded up pretty solid now," he told her as he slipped them on. "We ought to be all right here for a while. We have the gun and bullets, food and radio. Sooner or later, someone is bound to come and get us out."

Who you trying to reassure, Ben? Her, or yourself?

He picked up the rifle and began loading it.

In the background, the radio kept going on and on. *"...we join with law-enforcement agencies, urging you to seek shelter in a building, lock the doors and windows ..."*

"Hey, that's *us*," he said, half in jest, half in encouragement. "We're doing all right."

Barbra just sat there. Saying nothing, looking at nothing.

"... any suspicious strangers, and keep tuned to your radio and television for survival instructions, and further details of this continuing story ..."

At last, the gun was loaded and Ben turned to her once more. He had to keep trying, didn't he?

"Look ... I don't know if you're hearing me. But I'm going upstairs now."

No reaction.

"If anything should try to break in here, I can hear it from up there. I'll be down to take care of it."

Still nothing. It was as though she were still asleep, had never sat up.

"Everything is all right for now." He gestured around the room. "I'll be back to reinforce the windows and doors later. But you'll be all right for now. Okay?"

She still didn't say anything, but there was *some* kind of reaction this time — she blinked, her head trembled a bit. Her hair moved, and he could see the bruise he had left on her cheek.

Feeling a bit guilty for that, he reached out and touched her knee. "Okay?"

She said nothing, but he suspected she *was* hearing him after all.

Sighing, Ben stood and left the room, heading for the stairs.

As soon as he was gone, Barbra finished pulling her left hand out of her coat sleeve. She wasn't certain why she was ignoring him. Part of it was ire over his having slapped her, sure, but it was more than that. It was ... well, if she let on that she was doing better (a little better, anyway), he would expect her to start helping him again. And she wanted to, she really did, but she just couldn't take that pounding right now.

"*... civil defense officials in Cumberland have told newsmen that murder victims show evidence of having been ... partially* devoured *by their murderers ...*"

But then ... did she really want to be downstairs, alone?

At the top of the stairs, nearing the body with the chewed-off face, Ben had to stop and look away for a moment, fighting the urge to bend over and empty his guts. A blood-streaked pattern on the wall, looking almost like warped kanji, told him where the person had leaned before falling to die on the landing — whichever thing had attacked, and partially eaten, the previous owner of this house, Ben was just glad that it had wandered off.

The thought of getting any closer to the corpse, of touching it, was almost too much. But it had to be done.

Damn it, if he could drive a tire iron through a man's

forehead, he could do this.

Leaning the rifle against the wall, he stepped over the woman — he could see now that it was a woman, could tell from the clothing once he looked past the remains of her face, the hole in her temple — and, with precise, delicate movements, shifted her legs onto the rug with the rest of her. He then hefted one end of the rug, folding it so that he no longer had to look at her mutilated face, and dragged her down the hall toward the furthest possible room ...

"... consistent reports from witnesses to the effect that people who acted as though they were in a kind of trance were killing — *and* eating — *their victims, prompted authorities to examine the bodies of some of the victims."*

Barbra sat in her daze (a state which was becoming both frustrating and strangely comforting) and listened to the radio announcer. She could hear her companion moving around upstairs, but most of her attention, such as it was, focused on the radio.

"Medical authorities in Cumberland have concluded that in all cases, the killers are ... *eating the flesh* ... *of the people they murder."*

For the first time, Barbra considered that maybe this whole surreal night was nothing more than an elaborate nightmare (it was similar to Ben's earlier reckoning, but Barbra was less inclined to release the denial once she grabbed hold of it). That couldn't explain away the ache in her jaw where the man had slapped her, but it made more sense than any of the rest of it.

"... from Cumberland, Maryland, civil defense authorities have told newsmen that murder victims show evidence of having been partially devoured *by their murderers ..."*

Why, just listen to that. Think about it. People killing other people for no reason, and then *eating* them? It was ridiculous, absurd! Such things didn't happen, *couldn't* happen in the real world.

"*... shows conclusively that the killers* are *eating the flesh of the people they kill ...*"

She couldn't have been attacked in the cemetery, Johnny couldn't have *died* defending her. That in itself was preposterous — Johnny was far too selfish to have sacrificed himself in such a way. It was a funny notion, really.

Any moment now, she would wake up. Probably in the car with Johnny, having dozed off as they drove out to their father's grave — oh, Johnny would be so irritated. And for such a silly dream!

"*... this incredible story becomes more ghastly with each report,*" the radio announcer said, then went on to agree with her sentiments (which only made sense, since it was *her* dream), "*it's ... difficult to imagine such a thing actually happening ...*"

She heard some more knocking around, and wondered what in the world the man was doing up there. She should go tell him that he needn't bother, it was all just a dream.

Except ... this last knocking sound hadn't come from upstairs. It was much closer than that. Almost in the same room with her. From over near the old piano? Behind it? No, not there ...

Barbra turned in her seat, looking toward the dark door leading out into the hallway.

"*... but these are the reports we have been receiving and passing on to you, reports which have been* verified..."

The banging, which now sounded almost like footsteps, drifted from behind the door. But the door was open, resting almost flush to the wall. So ... what was making that noise?

Her breath came faster.

The radio told her, "*It* is *happening* ..."

Barbra recoiled. A hand appeared around the edge of the door.

The radio mocked her, "*No one is safe* ..."

The hand pushed the door forward. A young man in a short-sleeved shirt stepped from behind it, stepped right out of the wall.

Barbra screamed.

Ben heard her cry just as he emerged from the bedroom where he'd laid the dead woman. Hers, and what sounded like *men's* voices. So far as he knew, those things didn't talk, but that didn't slow him in the slightest as he grabbed the rifle and raced down the stairs, his heart pumping faster than his legs.

Ben burst into the room, and almost started firing away: Two men — a younger one holding Barbra by the arms; an older one wielding a broken slat from a bedframe like a cheap sword. They turned, saw Ben brandishing the rifle, and the younger one released Barbra and held up his hands.

"Hold it! Don't shoot!" the younger one cried, his eyes wide. Then, as though it explained everything, he added, "We're from town!"

The older one, a balding man with a bruise on one side of his shiny forehead, turned away from Ben, looking around. He blurted, "A radio!" and raced through the study doorway to kneel before it.

As Ben calmed down, his initial fear was replaced by anger. A sweep of the room revealed the small, nondescript open door that led into the wall near the corner by the piano and downward — he realized in an instant that these people had *not* breached his defenses, but had been here all along. He clenched his jaw, could practically feel the steam coming out of his ears. These bastards were lucky he didn't use the gun after all.

Looking at the younger one in disgust, he demanded, "How long you guys been down there? I could have used some help up here."

"That's the cellar," the older one answered as he fiddled with the radio. "It's the safest place."

"You mean you didn't hear the racket I was making up here?"

"How were *we* supposed to know what was going on?" the older man snapped back. "Could've been those *things* for all we knew."

Ben gestured at Barbra, who had withdrawn to the sofa once more. "That girl was screaming," he said, his disgust kicking up another notch. "Surely you must know what a girl screaming sounds like. Those *things* don't make any noise. *Anybody* would know that somebody had needed help!"

The younger man, his shirt stuck to his chest with sweat, finally spoke up. "Look, it's kinda hard to hear what's goin' on from down there."

"We thought we could hear screams," said the older one, still hunched before the radio, "but ... for all we knew that could've meant those things were in the house after her."

Ben sneered. "And you wouldn't come up and help."

The younger man was a lot more sensitive to Ben's derision than his comrade. "Well, if there were more of them—"

The older man cut him off, turning more of his stern attention to Ben. "The racket sounded like the place was being ripped apart. How were *we* supposed to know what was going on?"

"Now wait a minute," Ben returned. "You *just* got

finished saying you couldn't hear from down there. *Now* you say it sounded like the place was being ripped apart." He shook his head. "It would be nice if you'd get your story straight, man."

"All right," the older man said, his anger growing. "Now *you* tell *me* ..." He stood, gripping his own weapon and storming back toward Ben like a short, contentious bulldog — he was so hunched forward at the shoulders, his tie bulged out from where it was clipped to the front of his business shirt. "*I'm* not gonna take that kind of a chance when we've got a safe place. We luck into a safe place, and *you're* tellin' us we gotta risk our lives just because somebody might need help! Huh?!"

The man paced away from Ben, and suddenly Ben's ire deflated. In the face of selfishness at its bitter finest, what could he say? If a person viewed altruism as a detriment, would probably sneer at the notion of someone wanting to become, say, a teacher so that he could craft young minds and make the world a better place ... well, there was certainly nothing Ben could say that would change his mind. It made Ben more repelled by the man but less appalled, now that he could see what type of person he was dealing with.

"Yeah," he said at last in a low, tired voice. "Somethin' like that."

Again, the younger man proved more sensitive to Ben's tone. He stepped forward, saying, "All right, why don't we settle this—"

"Look, mister!" the older one cut him off again, reminding Ben more of a bulldog than ever. "We came up, okay? We're *here*! Now I suggest we *all* go back downstairs, before any of those things find out we're in here."

Ben dismissed him. "They can't get in here."

The younger man perked up. "You got the whole place boarded up?"

"Yeah, most of it. All but a few spots upstairs. They won't be hard to fix."

"You're insane!" the bulldog snapped. "The cellar is the safest place."

Ben felt his heat returning. "I'm telling you, they can't - get - in - here."

"And I'm telling you those things turned over our *car*! We were damned lucky to get away at all! Now *you* tell me those— those *things* can't get through this," he gestured around the room with his weapon, at all the boarded-up windows, "lousy pile of *wood*?!"

"His wife and kid's downstairs," the younger man said to Ben in a softer voice. "Kid's hurt."

Ben considered that; it made the bulldog's decisions a little more understandable, if not acceptable. He glanced at the bulldog, then turned away. "Well, I still think we're better off up here."

The younger man approached the bulldog, and indirectly gave Ben the bulldog's name. "We *could* strengthen everything up, Mister Cooper."

From across the room, Ben threw in, "With all of us working, we could fix this place up in no time! We have everything we need *up here*."

But the bulldog — Cooper — returned with, "We can take all that stuff *downstairs* with us." He shook his head. "Man, you're really crazy, you know that? You got a million windows up here! All these windows you're gonna— you're gonna make 'em strong enough to keep these things out, huh?"

"I told you, those things don't have any strength. I smashed three of them, and pushed another one out the door."

Cooper strode forward, gesturing at Ben with his weapon. "Did you hear me when I told you they turned over our *car*?"

"Oh, hell!" Ben snapped. "Any good five men could do that!"

"That's my point! Only there's not going to be five, or even ten ... there's gonna be twenty, thirty, maybe a *hundred* of those things. And as soon as they know we're here, this place is gonna be crawling with them."

Ben shrugged and strolled past him. "Well, if there're *that* many, they'll probably get us *wherever* we are."

Cooper sighed, then made what, for him, probably counted as an attempt to be civil. "Look ..." he glanced between Ben and the younger man, "... the cellar. The cellar, there's only one door, right? Just *one* door. That's all we have to protect. Tom and I fixed it so that it locks and boards from the inside. But up here, all these windows? Why, we'd never know where they were going to hit us next!"

Speaking of windows, Ben bent to peek outside between two of the boards he'd nailed up. He made a point of *not* looking at Cooper.

The younger man — *Tom*, Ben presumed — said, "You've got a point, Mister Cooper. But down in the cellar, there's no place to run to. I mean, if they *did* get in, there'd be no back exit. We'd be done for!"

Cooper grumbled and waved him off in classic curmudgeon fashion, stomping over to stand nearer the cellar door.

But Tom wasn't ready to give up yet. "We can get out of here, if we have to. And we got windows to see what's going on outside. But down there, with no windows, if a rescue party *did* come, we wouldn't even know it."

"But the cellar is the *strongest place*!" Cooper insisted.

Circling around Ben, who was mostly free now but still trying to get a clear shot, Tom saw that there were at least two of those things clambering at the window, their hands grasping, dirty fingernails clawing at his face even though he was too far back for them to possibly reach him.

Revulsion giving him strength, Tom hacked at one of them with the knife. He lashed out again and again, first cleaving into the back of the hand and then chopping whole fingers away — he didn't know if it made it better or worse that there was hardly any blood. By the time the thing finally withdrew its hand, it was little more than a butchered stump ...

... and yet the thing made no sound. Not a cry, not a moan, not even a grunt.

Even in the heat of the moment, with the things still grabbing at Ben and his rifle, that brought Tom up short. It didn't make sense! No matter what had happened to drive these people mad, no matter what had twisted and perverted them into actually *eating* their fellow human beings, how could any person — no matter how deranged — allow their own hand to be hacked, literally, *to pieces*?!

Even if they somehow felt *no pain* ... by God, the man's fingers were lying in a pile on the floor!

He glanced up at Ben, to see if he'd witnessed this impossible thing, but Ben had problems of his own to worry about.

Ben could not get a clear shot. Even when he pulled free, they were tugging at the barrel of the rifle — not as though they were trying to disarm him, but like they wanted him so much, they would grab any "part" of him and could not tell the difference. He would step back, dragging the weapon free, and then when he leaned in to take a shot, they would start grabbing at the barrel all over again.

He was still grateful to have the weapon, but at that

moment he would have traded anything for a *hand*gun.

Finally, everything lined up right, and he fired. The rifle was incredibly loud in the small kitchen, but he was gratified to see that he hit the thing right in the heart! One down, one to go ...

Except it *didn't* go down.

To Ben's disbelief, the thing staggered back several steps but did not fall. It stood still for a moment, staring down at the hole in its chest ... then it lifted its head and stared at him. No pain on its face, nothing in its eyes but that craving, that *hunger*.

That's not possible, Ben thought. *I mean, I know they're hard to stop when I'm slugging them with the tire iron, but ... Christ, I just shot it in the heart! In - the - heart!*

Was he losing his mind?

But Tom and even Cooper were seeing it, too. Tom leaned closer to him, almost huddling against him as they stared out the window at the thing that should have been lying dead or dying on the ground, but wasn't; Cooper stared from further away, grimacing so hard his teeth were grinding.

"Harry ...?!" called a distant, frightened woman's voice from somewhere in the house. Not Barbra's voice, so it had to be someone else from the cellar — Cooper's wife?

Sure enough, Cooper whispered a reply, "It's all right..." His voice was cracked and trembling, and for the first time, Ben sympathized with the man.

Of course, the woman couldn't possibly hear his quiet response, so she called again, "Harry, what's *happening*?!"

"It's ... it's all right!" Cooper called back louder this time, and his tone was anything but confident or reassuring.

The thing was back at the window again. Ben cocked the rifle and took aim for another shot. For several seconds, it was deja vu — the thing grabbing at the barrel of the gun; Ben split between pulling away and taking his shot.

Then he found another opening and took it.

This time he hit the thing on the right side of its chest. Not a heart shot, but the bullet had almost certainly ripped its lung to pieces, blasting particles of bone out through the shoulder blade. The trauma alone should have sent the thing into physical shock, even if it were too dumb to know when to lie down and die.

The thing looked at the second wound as it had the first, then, just as before, it lifted its gaze back to its prey.

Ben grumbled, "Damned thing ..." cocked the rifle, took careful aim while it was still away from the window, and fired again.

This time he hit it square in the forehead, pretty much the same spot where he'd driven the tire iron into the one with the torn throat.

It dropped like a rock, its brains and far too little blood collecting in a gooey pile in the grass around its head.

Third time's the charm.

Ben didn't know if that thought made him want to laugh or cry, but seeing the thing down and not moving made him almost giddy with relief ...

But unbeknownst to the refugees inside the house, this small victory had made their situation far worse.

Dozens had already wandered into the area, drawn by anything from instinct to forgotten routine to the echoes of Ben's hammering as he boarded up the house. Now, the rifle shots pulled them like iron fillings to a magnet.

Some of them were the hospital patients Ben had first seen at Beekman's Diner, having slowly but consistently shuffled their way in the direction he had driven the truck, long after their limited minds could remember why they had chosen this direction. Others were citizens from town; others were denizens of the local farms and neighboring properties.

Fully clothed or naked as the day they were born, nearly-pristine in appearance or the obvious victims of horrid assault, they drifted to the house. The gunshots had ceased, but their courses were set. They surrounded the place without conscious decision, some silent and tranquil, others agitated by the natural sounds of crickets and the still-present reverberations of thunder from the storm that had moved on.

One of them, a female, was drawn to movement on a nearby tree, barely visible in the light leaking from the house. It reached out and grasped the large insect, the lips of its burn-scarred face opening in a soft moan. It contemplated the bug for a few seconds, the wheels of its mind barely turning, then shoved the crawler into its mouth. It chewed, moaning — gasping, really — once again.

But no, it wasn't satisfied by this critter. What it wanted, what drew it with inexplicable but undeniable luxuria, was warm meat.

Human flesh.

In the house, Ben stormed past Cooper. "We've gotta fix these boards!"

"You're crazy!" Cooper returned, but he no longer sounded like a stubborn bulldog; he sounded like a frightened man. "Those things are gonna be at every window and door in this place! We've got to get down into the cellar!"

Be it because of the man's broken-record platform or because of his own fear, Ben lost it. "Go on down into your damn cellar!" he bellowed, waving Cooper away like the mongrel he was. "GET OUTTA HERE!"

Cooper looked back and forth around the room, flustered by Ben's outburst — like most bullies, he didn't know how to handle it when confronted by bigger bravado than his own. Finally, his eyes fell on Barbra, still sitting on the sofa, staring off into space as though a rifle hadn't just been fired three times not fifteen feet from her.

Cooper gestured at her. "I'm ... I'm taking the girl with me ..." He moved toward her, reaching out with one hand to take her by the arm.

Ben stepped forward. "You leave her here. You keep your hands off her, and everything else that's up here, too, because if I stay up here, I'm fighting for *everything* up here, and the radio and the food is part of what I'm fighting for! Now if you're going down to the cellar, *get!*" He waved Cooper away like a misbehaving dog again, turning back to the window.

Still floundering on uneven ground, Cooper turned to Tom. "The man's insane. He's *insane*. We've ... we've got to have food down there! We've got a *right!*"

That brought Ben around again. "This your house?"

"We've got a *right!*" Cooper repeated.

Ben also turned to Tom. "You going down there with him?"

Caught in the middle, Tom stammered, "W-well, I ... I—"

"Yes or no," Ben demanded, "this is your last chance — no beatin' around the bush!"

Tom looked back and forth, frozen with indecision.

Cooper turned back to Ben, and he was near pleading now. "L-L-Listen, I got a *kid* down there. Sh-She can't possib— I *couldn't* bring her up here, she can't possibly take all the racket from those, those things smashing through the windows."

"Well, you're her father," Ben answered, and

disappointed himself with the venom in his voice, venom he had always managed to avoid spitting at even the most rowdy of students ... and yet, he also found himself unable to resist it. "If you're *stupid* enough to go die in that trap, that's your business. However, I am *not* stupid enough to follow you." He paused as though considering his next words, even though he knew damn well what he was going to say. "It is tough for the kid that her old man is so *stupid*. Now ..." He shifted his grip on the rifle — he didn't point it directly at Cooper, but the message was clear. "Get the hell down in the cellar. You can be the boss down there ... I'm boss up here."

Cooper backed away, and the anger had returned to his eyes. No, not anger this time — *hatred*. He gripped his own weapon, holding it in front of him. "You *bastards*."

Ben pointedly turned his back on Cooper.

"You know I won't open this door again," Cooper warned. "I mean it."

Tom took one more shot at playing peacekeeper. "Mister Cooper, with your help, we could—"

" 'With - my - *help*'!" Cooper spat back.

"Let him go, man," Ben said to Tom. "His mind is made up. Just let him *go!*"

Cooper glowered at them both, grinding his teeth and stopping just short of *growling* at them, then turned on his heel and headed for the basement door.

Tom looked from Ben to Cooper, then realized that Cooper was actually going to do it, he was going to return to the basement and lock the door. "Wait a minute!" he called.

Cooper barely slowed down, so Tom reached out and grabbed him by the arm and, with surprising assertion, pulled him back. He stepped into the doorway himself and called down, "Judy? Come on up here."

Judy? Ben thought. Since Ben could assume Tom wasn't calling for either Cooper's wife or daughter, that meant he was asking someone *else* to join them. How many people were down there? He hadn't even thought to ask.

A timid young girl climbed the stairs into view — younger than Barbra; hell, she looked almost young enough to be one of Ben's students. She wore a denim jacket and blue jeans, and sandals that weren't much more practical than Barbra's stockinged feet.

As she emerged from the cellar, Cooper pointed at her and said to Tom, "You're gonna let them get *her*, too, huh?"

The timid girl — Judy — looked at Cooper, then at Ben (and his gun).

"It's all right, hon," Tom said to her in a low voice, pushing her with a gentle hand past Cooper, "go ahead."

Ben watched as Judy floated over near Barbra and perched tentatively on the arm of the sofa, and as Cooper, without another word, disappeared into the cellar stairwell, slamming the door. A moment later, they all heard Cooper — as Ben was sure was his intention — barricading the door behind him.

Forever the optimist, Tom leaned against the outside of the door. "If we stick together, man, we can fix it up real good. There ... there's lots of places we can run to up here." Nothing from Cooper but the sound of more boards sliding into place. "Mister Cooper, we'd all be a lot better off if all three of us were working *together*."

Silence was his only reply.

Leaving Tom to his wishful thinking, Ben crossed the room to the sofa, where Barbra had barely moved and had said nothing since he rushed downstairs to find Tom trying to reason with her.

"Yeah?!" Tom replied.

Harry stared at Helen, but he still didn't say anything, and she was more than happy to take advantage of his indecision.

"If Judy would come downstairs for a few minutes," she hollered, looking at her husband and daring him to overrule her, "Harry and I could come upstairs."

"Okay, yeah!" Tom answered, sounding pleased. "Right away!"

Harry looked down, his lips pressed so tight that his mouth disappeared into a thin line — he looked like a sulking child.

Helen elected not to voice that particular observation...

On the ground floor, Tom walked over to Judy where she sat on the arm of the sofa. Bending forward, hands on his thighs, he asked, "Will you do it?"

Anxious, she asked, "Do I have to?" She had been a nervous wreck when they separated before and she wasn't in a hurry to leave his side again — with those deranged people running around, she didn't want to let him out of her sight!

"Look, honey," he reasoned, "nothing's gonna get done with them down there and us up here." He touched her shoulder. "Do this. For me."

Judy sighed. "Okay."

Tom returned to the basement door. "Okay! Open up."

Judy followed him, her stride less than enthusiastic.

Cooper opened the door and Judy stepped inside. He stared at her, but she was relieved that he did not rant this time like he had before. She didn't like him very much, but she *did* like his wife, and it was as much for her as for Tommy that she descended those dark stairs once again.

She found Missus Cooper holding her sick daughter's

hand, that poor little girl. Seeing those fever-dampened locks gave her another reason to go along with this exchange.

"I'll take good care of her, Helen," she said, barely remembering to call the older woman by her first name.

Missus Cooper nodded, but did not stand up immediately. She stroked her daughter's left arm — the good one, the one that hadn't been bitten by that crazy woman. Finally, she said in a low voice, "She's all I have."

Judy wasn't sure how to respond to that. She could tell that the Coopers did not share a happy marriage, and felt (strangely enough) almost *guilty* for the strong bond she had with Tommy. Instead, she settled for, "Why don't you go upstairs now?"

Missus Cooper patted her daughter's good arm, stood, offered Judy a weak smile, then headed for the stairs.

Judy took her post, adjusting Karen's blanket and sitting at her side, but the little girl gave no acknowledgment of her presence or her mother's departure...

Harry exited the cellar first, looking around as though he half-expected the lunatics to have already broken through every nook and cranny. His hands clenched and unclenched, his fingers performing a nervous little dance, feeling for the weapon he was no longer carrying. He looked back at Helen, and tried to put some fire into it.

You see? he tried to say with his eyes. *You see how dangerous it is up here? You see why I hustled us down into the cellar in the first place? You see that I'm right?!*

But all Helen saw was his fear. And she realized that Harry wasn't all bluster this time, wasn't *just* wanting to prove himself right over everyone else. That might have been a part of it (he was Harry, after all), but he was sincerely, deeply *afraid* to be up here. He honestly did think the cellar was safer, really was trying, in his harsh way, to protect his family as best he could.

Then he turned away and stalked across the room to inspect the boarded windows. Helen started to follow him, but then she noticed the young woman on the sofa. Not much older than Judy, the blonde woman was slumped so far over she was almost lying on her side. She was running her fingers over the doily on the arm of the sofa, seemed fascinated by it — which, given the situation they were all in, sent up a warning flag to Helen right away.

Then Tom stepped forward and confirmed her suspicions. "Her brother was killed."

Before Helen could reply, a voice called from elsewhere in the house, "Hey! Give me a hand with this thing!"

Tom apologized, "I gotta go help Ben with the television," before leaving the room.

Harry was still running his inspection tour, so Helen approached the young woman ... but then stopped short. She had intended to join her on the sofa, but the girl's obsessive focus on every intricate detail of the embroidery made her a little nervous. How would the girl react if Helen just plunked herself down right next to her?

Instead, Helen sat in a nearby chair. She would try to talk to the girl first, before getting too close to her. Except she wasn't certain what to *say*.

So she sat in the rickety chair and watched the blonde girl. Watched her run her fingers over the doily, tracing every line, every curve. Helen soon found herself fidgeting with her wedding ring, and decided that she needed a cigarette. God, did she need one!

Pulling a pack from her coat pocket, she struck a match and lit up. Funny enough, while the blonde had ignored Harry's tramping around and Helen's creaking chair, she looked over right away when the match sparked to life. At first glance, her expression came across as rather bland, but upon closer inspection, Helen decided that the young woman was actually riding along the edge of a precipice. She was terrified beyond her ability to process it.

Having seen one of those lunatics take a bite — a *bite*! — out of her daughter's arm, Helen could understand why.

"Don't be afraid of me," she said in a soft voice. "I'm Helen Cooper. Harry's wife."

The blonde just stared. Had Harry bothered to introduce himself before? Probably not. But then she realized that the young woman was staring at something specific — her still-burning match.

Helen shook the match out, and as soon as the flame died, the blonde lost her focus. She turned back to the doily.

Then Harry clomped back into the room. "This place is ridiculous! Look at this!" He marched over to one of the windows. "There's a million weak spots up here." He tugged on one of the boards, which did indeed give some under his grasp.

Then he spotted Helen's cigarette and hustled over to her side. "Give me one of those." He yanked the pack from his wife's hand — she gave him a dirty look for his rude behavior, then realized that the only witness to it wasn't exactly paying attention.

Harry glanced at the blonde as he lit his own cigarette, and she relayed, "Her brother was killed."

Harry thought about that for a moment, then nodded as though to say, *Sure he was, whatever.* All that was missing was a shrug.

Helen looked away from her callous husband.

Then he sighed and was off again, pacing around the room. "And they talk about these windows. I can't see a damn thing!" He turned back toward Helen, still pleading his case. "There could be fifteen *million* of those things out there. That's how much good these *windows* are."

Then Harry was pacing, pacing and smoking. He was behind her, mostly, so she couldn't see him, but she could *feel* him. Finally, she snapped, "Why don't you do something to *help* somebody?!"

Harry ignored her, but she knew damn well he'd heard her.

Then Tom and the other man — "Ben," she thought Tom had called him — appeared, carrying a large, old television set into the room.

"I have it," Ben told Tom. "Drag a couple of those chairs together."

Tom hurried to do so, excited — Helen noticed that even the blonde sat up and paid attention. Tom grabbed two chairs, then said, "There's a socket over here," and placed them opposite the sofa.

Grunting from exertion, Ben lowered the television into place and reached behind it to plug it in.

Harry moved around until he was near the sofa. Out of nowhere, he bent over the blonde woman and said, "Now you'd better watch this, and try to understand what's going on."

Ben straightened up behind the television and gave Harry a dark look.

Harry threw his arms into the air; half-exasperation, half-*I wasn't doin' nothin'!* "I don't want anyone's life on *my* hands."

Embarrassed, Helen asked, "Is there anything *I* can do to hel—"

But Harry's attitude had already set Ben off. He stood, fuming, and pointed at Harry. "I don't want to hear any more from you, mister. If you stay up here, you take orders from *me*! And that includes leaving the girl *alone*!"

Then Tom drew all of their attention to the television. "It's on. It's on!"

"There's no sound," Harry pointed out in typical Harry-fashion.

Tom turned more of the old-style dials.

"Play with the rabbit ears," Harry instructed.

Ben stepped around and touched them, and after a few short bursts, the sound synced up to the image.

Not that there was much to see. The anchorman — no one famous or familiar, just a bespeckled talking-head who had been available at the time everything went to hell — sat reading copy as other employees bustled around in the background and machines rattled away noisier than usual.

"*... incredible as they seem,*" the anchorman was saying, "*are* not *the results of mass hysteria.*"

" 'Mass hysteria'," Harry scoffed. "What, do they think we're *imagining* all this?!"

"Shut up!" Ben shouted, and Helen grew keenly aware of the rifle in the man's hands; not that she could blame him for his frustration with Harry — she wanted to tape his big mouth shut, too!

Ben pulled a chair around to the front side of the television, and then everyone in the room settled in and fell silent.

"*The wave of murder which is sweeping the eastern third of the nation,*" the anchorman told them, "*is being committed by creatures who feast upon the flesh of their victims.   First eyewitness accounts of this grisly development came from people who were understandably frightened and almost incoherent.   Officials, and newsmen, at first discounted those eyewitness description as being beyond belief.   However, reports persisted. Medical examinations of some of the victims bore out the fact that they had been partially devoured.*"

Helen looked at Harry. She thought of that *bitch* taking a bite out of their little girl's arm. If they hadn't gotten away ... she shuddered to think about it.

But none of them said anything; they huddled closer to the television.

"*I think we have some late word, now just arriving, and ...*" the anchorman leaned back to take some sheets of paper from one of his colleagues, "*... I interrupt to bring this to you.*" The anchorman read the top sheet, pausing before he continued, "*This is the latest disclosure in a report from National Civil Defense headquarters in Washington. It has been established that persons who have recently* died ... *have been returning to* life, *and committing acts of murder. Wide-spread investigation of reports from funeral homes, morgues, and hospitals, has concluded that the unburied dead are coming* back to life, *and seeking human victims.*"

A deep chill ran through them all. Each of them, even Barbra in her inhibited way, thought about what they had experienced this night — Barbra, the man in the cemetery; Ben, Beekman's Diner; Tom, the lake; the Coopers, their assault on the road — and it finally made sense.

Except that it *didn't* make "sense" at all, not in any way! They were under siege by the *living dead*? Their collective perception of reality was being blown to bits by silent, staggering bombs, the fallout leaving them speechless.

And yet ... hadn't each of them, especially Ben, already considered this possibility, however *im*possible, far back in the depths of their minds? The way these things moved, the way they looked, the way they smelled, that empty, inhuman hunger in their eyes — and don't forget how difficult it was to stop them, how one of them kept coming even after being *shot through the heart*!

None of them had voiced these suspicions before, not even to themselves, and they said nothing to each other now, did not even exchange looks of disbelief. They just ... listened.

The anchorman had paused again, looking uncomfortable — almost embarrassed. *"It's hard for us here to ... believe what we're reporting to you, but it does seem to be a fact."* He fell silent once more, then took a deep, steadying breath and continued, *"When this emergency first began, radio and television were advising people to stay inside, behind locked doors, for safety. That situation has now changed — we're able to report a definite course of action. Civil defense machinery has been organized to provide rescue stations with food, shelter, medical treatment, and protection by armed National Guardsmen."*

At this, text appeared at the bottom of the screen: <u>Youngstown</u> — Township Municipal Hospital

"Stay tuned to the broadcasting stations in your local area for this list of rescue stations. This list will be repeated throughout our news coverage."

More text: <u>Sharon</u> — Central Fire Department

"Look for the name of the rescue station nearest you, and make your way to that location as soon as possible..."

Ben, having finally regained his speech, turned to the group. "So we have that truck; if we can get some gas, we can get out of here."

Tom said, "There's a pump out by the shed!"

"I know," Ben said in frustration, "that's why I pulled in here. But it's *locked*."

The text at the bottom of the screen now read: <u>Mercer</u> — Municipal Building And it continued to change as the news marched on.

The anchorman continued, "... *called this afternoon by the President. Since convening, this conference of the Presidential Cabinet, the FBI, the Joint Chiefs of Staff, and the CIA, has not produced any public information.*

"Why are space experts being consulted about an Earthbound emergency?"

Now the group did exchange glances. Space experts? Ben vaguely recalled that NASA had been mentioned on the radio earlier, but he had been so focused on boarding up the house, he had tuned most of it out by that point.

"So far, all the betting on the answer to that question centers on the recent explorer satellite shot to Venus. That satellite, you'll recall, started back to Earth but never got here — as the space vehicle which orbited Venus and then was purposely destroyed by NASA, when scientists discovered it was carrying a mysterious, high-level radiation with it.

"Could that radiation be somehow responsible for the wholesale murders we're now suffering?"

I doubt that, Ben mused. He was no expert, but he knew enough from teaching the odd science class that, whatever the source, hard radiation would *destroy* flesh before doing anything so bizarre as to *reanimate* it. It was a ludicrous theory.

Have you got a better one, smartass?

No. He didn't.

Ben suddenly realized that Cooper had risen from the sofa and was now hovering just over his shoulder. He latched onto his irritation, as it was something familiar and known, and had nothing to do with the dead attacking the living. He said, "It's obvious our best move is to try to get out of here."

Cooper returned, "How are you gonna get over to that pump?"

Before Ben could answer, Tom blurted, "Look!"

On the television, the image had cut from the newsroom to the field, where a group of reporters were hustling after some high-ranking military officer, accompanied by two men in suits, as he strode down the sidewalk. Both the radio and television had reiterated "Washington" more than once, but this footage appeared to be taking place in daylight, so Ben assumed that it was being shot somewhere on the west coast — perhaps Washington State?

One reporter got in closer than the others. He asked, "*You're coming from a meeting regarding the explosion of the Venus probe, is that right?*"

The officer gave the grudging answer, "*Uh, yes ... yes, that was the, uh, subject of the meeting.*"

"*Do you feel there is a connection between this and the—*"

The officer started to answer in the negative, but one of the suits with him, a balding, bearded man, answered, "*There's a definite connection. A* definite *connection.*" This earned him a hostile look from the military man.

The reporter pushed, "*In other words, you feel that the radiation on the Venus probe is enough to cause these mutations?*"

"*There was a very high degree of radiation—*"

The officer broke back in, though he sounded no more confident than before. "*Just a minute. Uh, I'm not sure that that's certain at all. I don't think that has been, uh...*"

Now the other suit, a shorter man in an overcoat, spoke. The reporter had to redirect his microphone, so all that really came through was, "*... explanation that we have at this time.*"

The officer now gave *that* man an exasperated look — regardless of his rank, he did not appear to be in command here, and it clearly frustrated him.

From the reporter, "*In other words, it is the military's viewpoint that the radiation is* not *the cause of the mutation?*"

Trapped, the officer stopped walking and replied, "*I can't speak for the entire military at this time, gentlemen.*"

"*It seems to be—*"

"*I must disagree with these gentlemen,*" the officer clarified, "*presently, until we, uh, until this is* irrefutably *proved.*"

The shorter suit, looking very tired, spoke up again. "*Everything is being done that can be done.*"

The officer pointed across the intersection. "*We'll have to hurry for our next meeting.*"

The report from the field continued for a while longer, but it all boiled down to more of the same: The reporters followed and hounded the three men with the same questions; the officer and his two companions agreed and disagreed and agreed to disagree; and as they reached their car, they signed off with more promises that they were doing "everything possible to solve the problem."

Cooper stood and turned away, visibly disgusted.

Ben didn't blame him. "We've heard all these. No, we have to try to get out of here."

Helen spoke up. "He said the rescue stations had doctors and medical supplies." She looked to her husband. "If we could get Karen there, we could get *help* for her."

On the screen, as the anchorman rattled on, the latest text rolled over to: <u>Willard</u> — Willard Medical Center

"Willard," Ben said. The name nagged at him for a brief moment, then he got it. "I saw a sign that said 'Willard'."

Tom nodded. "It's only about seventeen miles from here."

Ben stood and turned to him. "You know this area? You from around here?"

"Judy and I are both from around here. We were on our way up to the lake to go swimming. Judy had a radio, and we heard the first reports about this ..." Tom started to tell them about what they had seen, about the man biting off his wife's lips, but he decided not to go into it. What would it help to relive *that* again? "... so, we knew the old house was here, and we came in. Found the lady upstairs, dead. Then these other people came. We went down into the basement and put a bar across the door, and it *is* pretty strong."

"How could we possibly get away from here?" Cooper asked his wife and the room at large. "We've got a sick child, two women, one woman out of her *head*, three men, and the place is surrounded."

Helen, for her part, turned away from him, back toward the television. The anchorman was interviewing a Doctor Grimes in the news studio. At first, it just seemed like more of the same — a detailed explanation of how *little* anyone knew of what was going on. But then something the doctor said jumped out at her, and caused her stomach to drop down into her feet.

"... *yes, we have some answers,*" the doctor was saying. "*But first, let me stress the importance of seeking medical attention for anyone who's been injured in any way. We don't know yet what complications might result from such injuries ...*"

Ben heard it, too. "How bad has your kid been hurt?" he asked her.

"Oh ... she ..." Helen was suddenly at a loss for words. She realized, of course, that something was wrong with Karen. She wanted so much to blame it on shock, but the fact was that the bite on her arm was terribly infected —

the human mouth was filthy, filled with germs, but the speed of the infection already scared her ... and that was before the television explained what exactly those *things* really were.

When Ben realized that she didn't have a ready answer for him, he said, "Look ... you go down there and tell ..." He glanced back at Tom. "Was her name 'Judy'?" Tom nodded. "Yeah, you tell Judy to come up here, and you stay with the kid. All right?"

Helen didn't argue — she *wanted* to be at her daughter's side now.

As she stood and headed for the basement door, Ben turned back to the television.

"*... in the cold room at the university,*" Doctor Grimes was saying, "*we had a cadaver. A cadaver from which all four limbs had been amputated. Sometime early this morning, it opened its eyes and began to move its trunk. It was* dead*, but it opened its eyes and tried to move ...*"

Back in the cellar, Helen found herself rushing to her daughter's side.   That note about seeking medical assistance had rattled her, badly.

"They want you upstairs." She touched Judy on the arm, then looked at Karen. "Did she ask for me?"

Judy moved so that Helen could sit down. "She hasn't said anything."

Helen patted her daughter's forearms, mindful of the bandage on her right arm that was partially soaked with blood.

Or was that blood and pus*?*

Shut up!

"I don't understand," Helen said aloud. She leaned forward, forcing herself to smile. "Baby? It's Mommy."

Karen opened her eyes long enough to say, "I hurt ..." She cringed in pain, and it stabbed straight into Helen's heart, her soul.

Judy patted Helen on the back. "I'll come back down as soon as I find out what they want."

Helen nodded as she walked away. "Thank you, Judy." But it wouldn't matter, because she wouldn't leave her daughter's side again. Not if she could help it. Not until they were ready to carry her out of this God-forsaken place and take her to get some real help.

So Helen Cooper sat with her daughter and vehemently ignored the pungent smell wafting up from her infected wound ...

On the television, Doctor Grimes continued on as more rescue stations were identified in the text below him. "...*the body should be disposed of at once, preferably by cremation.*"

The anchorman asked, "*Well how long after death, then, does the body become reactivated?*"

"*It's only a matter of minutes,*" the doctor said, dour.

" '*Minutes'? Well, that doesn't give people time to make any arrangeme—*"

"*No, you're right, it doesn't give them time to make funeral arrangements. The bodies must be carried to the street and ...*" The doctor hesitated, briefly, showing the first real emotion since appearing in the news studio. "...*and burned. They must be burned* immediately. *Soak them with gasoline and burn them.*"

The anchorman looked away, again appearing embarrassed. But he said nothing, made no accusations against the doctor's harsh assertions.

The doctor continued, sounding colder now, perhaps in self-castigation for his moment of weakness. "*The bereaved will have to forego the dubious comforts that a funeral service will give. They're just dead flesh, and dangerous.*"

Judy arrived just in time to hear this last bit — not having been present for the earlier announcement, it confused her more than upset her.

Then Ben noticed her and began issuing instructions. "Look, I need you to find some bedspreads or sheets to tear up into small strips, okay?"

Judy nodded.

Ben turned to Tom. "Is there a *fruit* cellar here?"

"... Yes."

"We need some bottles or jars, to make Molotov Cocktails, hold them off while we try to escape."

Tom got the idea. "Hey! There's a big can of kerosene down there."

Judy said, "I'll see what I can find."

Tom agreed, "I'll look for the bottles."

The growing sense of camaraderie prompted Cooper to finally participate. "There's a big key ring down there," he said, still sounding reluctant. "There may be a key to the gas pump on it."

"I'll check," Tom said before heading down, though he said it more to Ben than to Harry Cooper.

Ben looked at the man for a moment, then said, "You can toss the cocktails from a window upstairs. Meantime, a couple of us can go out and try to get the gas, then come back for the rest of the people."

"But that'll leave a door open someplace!"

Ben chose to overlook his belligerent tone, this time. "Yeah, that's right. It better be this door." He walked over to the front door of the house. "It's closer to the truck." He looked back toward the cellar. "Before we go out, we put some supplies behind the cellar door — while we're gone, the rest of you can hole up in there."

Before Cooper could reply, Tom emerged, carrying a box. "I found some fruit jars in the cellar." He put the box down on one of the chairs, then held up a largish, mostly naked key ring. "And there's a key on here that's labeled for the gas pump out back."

Ben thought for a moment, plotting in all out in his mind. Then he was forced to admit, "I, I'm not really that used to the truck. I found it abandoned."

"Abandoned," yeah. That's one way to describe it, Ben.

Shush, I don't have time for that right now.

Tom stepped forward. "*I* can handle the truck, no sweat."

Ben considered that. After thrusting himself into the defacto leadership position, he found it uncomfortable to delegate such an important task to someone else. But then, just as he had been insisting all along, their chances were best if they all worked together — himself, Tom, even Cooper.

Ben fished the truck keys out of his pocket and handed them over. "You're it, then. You and I'll go."

Tom accepted the keys; his face paled somewhat as the reality of what he had just volunteered for soaked in — leaving the protection of the house, going outside with all of those *dead* people who wanted to eat him. His eyes widened and fresh sweat glistened on his forehead, but he said nothing.

Ben met Tom's gaze, then addressed Cooper. "We'll put whatever lumber we find behind the cellar door. You can go upstairs and toss the cocktails from a window." Cooper looked like he was on the verge of asking a question, but Ben turned back to the younger man before he had a chance. "Tom, you and I'll have to unboard this door." Then he returned his attention to Cooper without pausing, "After you toss the cocktails, you hustle back down here and *lock* this door. It's no good to board it up, because we'll have to get back in quickly."

To his credit, Cooper nodded — he looked very nervous about the whole idea, but he didn't argue; it was the closest to being a "team player" that Ben had yet seen from the man.

This prompted Ben to lower his voice, which he belatedly realized had gotten a little too loud — Cooper wasn't the only nervous one here. "After we get the gas and back into the house ... *then* we'll worry about getting everybody into the truck."

More nods all around.

"Now let's move it."

Ben headed off to prepare. Cooper stood where he was, staring at the door they would soon be opening. He hated feeling so helpless, so out of control — *God*, did he hate it! But no one was listening to *him*, so he had no choice but to go along with Ben's decisions, for now.

The television played on, hammering their situation home.

"... rescue stations being set up. Indication are that, before this emergency is over, we will need many, many more such rescue stations ..."

In the study, Judy sat with the scissors in her hand, held so tight that her palm was sweating. Unlike the others, who had tuned out the television by this point, she was still able to hear it, and she had been listening. She had heard their recapping of the nature of those sick people out there — except that "sick" no longer covered it, did it? — and she was putting up a valiant fight against full-fledged panic. Judy envied the blonde woman on the sofa in the next room, who appeared to have checked-out in order to escape having to deal with this. *She* was the lucky one; Judy didn't have that luxury.

And then the reason she didn't have that luxury walked

into the room: Tommy.

He entered with a plate and a mason jar filled with water; he carried them to the desk before sitting and turning to face her. He must have known that, on top of listening to the television reports, she had *also* overheard the plan that would send him outside.

But the moment she realized she had his attention, she reached deep within herself and found just what she knew he needed.

"You always have a smile for me," he marveled, his voice soft in that way she loved so much. "How can you smile like that, all the time?"

Then, in spite of her best effort, her smile began to slip, and Tommy looked away before it collapsed altogether.

"How many do you have done?" he asked, pouring some of the water from the jar into the plate — only the fumes that arose told her that she'd been wrong; it wasn't water, it was kerosene.

She handed him the small pile of strips she had cut so far.

Counting the few that were there, he shook his head and admonished her, "Come on, honey, we gotta move."

As she watched him wetting the strips, desperate butterflies fluttered in her stomach. "Tom, are you *sure* about the phone?"

"The phone is dead *out*."

Defeated, she sighed. "If I could only call the folks. They're going to be so worried about us ..."

He gave her his full attention. "Everything will be all right. As soon as we get to Willard, we'll call them — they might even be there."

She nodded, but it wasn't very convincing. "I know..."
He returned to his work, and so did she. Or she *tried* to.

She had barely gotten a single clip out of the scissors before speaking up again. "Tom?"

This time he kept his eyes on his work, barely grunting in acknowledgment.

"Are you *sure* we're doing the right thing, Tom?"

"What, about gettin' outta here?"

"Yeah."

"Well ... the television said that's the right thing to do." He considered it a moment longer, then said with more confidence, "We've *got* to get to a rescue station."

"I don't know ..."

"Come on, honey, you're starting to sound like Mister Cooper now."

She grew more agitated. "But why do *you* have to go out there?"

"Look, *I* know how to handle that truck. And I can handle the pump. Ben doesn't know anything about that stuff." Tom actually had no idea if that were true or not, but he felt he had to say it for her sake.

Unfortunately, Judy looked anything but convinced. "But we're safe in here."

"For how *long*, honey?" he asked. Distraught, she moved off the chair and onto the floor in front of him — for a terrifying moment, Tom thought she was going to *beg* him not to go outside. So he pushed on in a rush, "We're safe *now*, but there's gonna be more and more of those things."

"I know," she said, almost snapping for the first time, "I *know* all that."

He began to flounder — the truth was, *he* didn't want to go outside any more than she wanted him to. But his gut instincts told him that Ben was right and Mister Cooper was wrong. It was like his old civics teacher used to say — they had to remain *pro*active, not *re*active; they had to make their own chances, not take what was given to them. Because since he'd seen that guy bite his wife's lips off at the lake—

No. No, he wouldn't think about that. He had to focus on Judy now, make Judy feel better, more confident, even if he did not.

"Honey, listen," he said, and he wished he could keep the fear out of his voice. "Remember when we had the big flood? Remember how difficult it was for us to convince you that it was *right* to leave?"

She nodded, sort of. And she wasn't looking at him now, just staring down at the floor.

He pressed on. "Remember— remember we had to go to Willard *then*?"

When she didn't respond at all this time, he slipped off his chair and joined her on the floor, down on the same level.

"Well *this* isn't a passing thing, honey. It— it's not like, just, a wind passing through. We've got to *do* something, and *fast*."

Finally, she looked up at him through the curtain of her long, beautiful hair ... and then she threw herself forward, wrapping her arms around his neck, and held him. She gasped a couple of times, and he thought she was near tears, but then she said, "I ... I just don't want *you* to go out there. That's all."

"Hey ... Smiley ..." He was fighting against his own tears now. "Where's that big smile for me?"

She said nothing, and certainly didn't pull back to smile for him. She just held him so tight.

"Boy ..." he said, trying for humor, however feeble. "You're sure no use at all, are ya?"

Still nothing from Judy, not even a twinge, and certainly no laugh or giggle.

"We've got work to do, honey. And you ..." His voice threatened to crack. He wouldn't cry now, not in front of Judy — he wouldn't! He pulled away, struggling to free himself from her death grip. "You ..."

She let go, pulled back, looked into his eyes, and all of his secrets were revealed. He had nothing left to say, no more assurances to offer.

So he kissed her ...

A time later (but not *enough* time, as far as Judy was concerned), the work was done and she found herself back in the living room, sitting on the arm of the sofa again next to the blonde, Barbra, who had still barely said two words to anyone.

Mister Cooper emerged from his cellar (that's how Judy thought of it now; *his* cellar) just as Ben brought over a box full of the Molotov cocktails.

Mister Cooper accepted the box from him — he'd become a lot more agreeable, and Judy suspected Missus Cooper had something to do with that — then turned toward the sofa. For a moment, Judy thought he was going to say something to her, but then he pointed past her, toward Barbra. "We better get her downstairs," he said to Ben.

Judy took the cue. She said to the other woman, "We have to go downstairs now, Barbra."

But Barbra didn't budge or reply; instead, she looked to Ben for confirmation.

"She's right," Ben assured her as he knelt in front of the sofa as before. "You have to go downstairs now, just for a little while, until we get back."

Still nothing but a blank stare from Barbra.

So Ben added, "Then we can all *leave*."

That got the reaction he was hoping for — Barbra brightened. "Oh, I'd *like* to leave. *Yes*."

Ben reach out for her, and she accepted his hand. He pulled her to her feet, and once she was moving, she headed toward the cellar door on her own. Judy collected Barbra's coat, then nodded to Ben and followed after her.

Once Ben saw that they were indeed on their way, he joined Tom over by the front door. Cooper lingered in the room a moment longer, cast a longing glance toward the cellar, then hefted the box of jars and headed for the stairway without a word — grudging or not, he knew what his job was, and Ben was relieved that he was going to do it.

Ben set the rifle down next to the door, and Tom offered him the hammer. Ben hesitated — *Were they really going to do this? Go back outside?* — then accepted the tool, took a deep breath, and said, "Good luck."

"Yeah ..." Tom agreed.

And then they were unboarding the door.

It didn't take long, but it was a lot noisier than either of them would have preferred. However many of those things were on this side of the house, this would surely draw their attention, and maybe bring a few more from the back as well. It was disheartening to see how quickly such hard work could be dismantled, but they were committed now.

Across the room, Judy peeked from around the still-open cellar door. Tom noticed as he turned to toss aside some of the wood, and their gazes locked. To his everlasting amazement, she offered him another of her beautiful smiles, and that smile both emboldened him and almost stole his nerve.

Upstairs, Cooper set the mason jars on a table beside one of the front windows, then folded first one then the other curtain up and over the rod. This whole plan was insane enough as it was — the last thing he wanted to do was set the house on fire!

Opening the window, he knocked the storm screen outward, letting it fall wherever it may. It had gotten so dark outside, he couldn't be sure how many of those things lingered in front of the house, but he could *smell* them all the way up here, which meant there were a lot.

A lot of *dead* people.

He fought back a shudder, shoving that thought from his mind. If he was going to think about anything, it would be Karen, and Helen.

Carefully, he opened the box and removed the first mason jar, and strove to ignore the gasps and soft groans that rose up from the yard below.

At the front door, Ben returned with another of his tried-and-true custom torches. The smoke was as bad as before, and he bellowed, "You ready upstairs?!" which startled the hell out of Tom and Judy.

"Yeah!" came Cooper's voice.

"Okay, *toss 'em!*"

At the upstairs window, Cooper struck a match and lit the cloth-fuse of the first jar. He was unnerved by how fast the flame caught, and he wasted no time hurling the jar outside. It struck the ground to the front-left of the truck — dear God, if he had tossed the jar any harder, he might have hit it!

But it had the desired effect: The creatures — and there *were* a lot more of them now — immediately withdrew, the closest ones throwing their arms before their eyes as though the eight-foot wide circle of flames were a lot hotter and brighter than it really was. Their moans elevated in both volume and pitch as they retreated in fear.

Cooper didn't wait. He lit the second jar, but took the extra second to make sure that he hit the ground to the front-right of the truck. The things withdrew further, leaving both truck doors free for Ben and Tom to reach.

But Cooper wasn't satisfied. To his surprise, he found himself getting a morbid *thrill* from this — striking back at the bastards who hurt his little girl! He threw a third and then a fourth jar, pushing the things further back, and the last jar spilled its flames right onto the legs of one of them!

To Cooper's obscene pleasure, the burning creature danced around next to the truck. It was really moaning now, they all were, but even though it was actually *on fire*, the cries still smacked more of fear than of pain — its clothes, its *skin* was burning, and yet it didn't go down anymore than the one Ben had shot in the heart.

My God ... it's true. They really are dead.

He had seen enough. He bolted for the stairway.

Reaching the ground floor, he rounded into the hallway and called out, "Go ahead! Go on!"

Judy watched from the cellar doorway as Tom unlocked the front door, then ran outside with Ben right on his heels.

Tom hauled ass, practically flying off the front porch — Ben followed at a slower pace, the torch burning in one hand and the rifle ready in the other. As Tom dashed for the driver's side of the truck, he saw that one of the things, its clothes in disarray and its sunken eyes dark against its pale face, had wandered around the fires and into his direct path. He didn't see any choice but to take the dead man head on.

Slamming into it, he expected it to bowl over backwards. Instead, this one surprised him with its strength and coordination; it closed its arms, grabbing him by the shoulders.

God, the smell! Even if the television hadn't revealed the true nature of these maniacs, this one's stench alone would have given it away. The reek made Tom want to vomit.

For a moment, they danced in twisted intimacy, then Tom regained some leverage and shoved it away — it ripped the sleeve of his T-shirt, while he tore *its* shirt halfway off its body. Tom spun and yanked the truck's door open, but the thing was on him again before he could climb into the driver's seat. He braced himself and rammed his foot into its stomach, which finally knocked it to the ground. But there was another one right behind it, and Tom just barely pulled the door closed in time.

On the other side of the truck, Ben waited for Tom to get the engine started. He didn't know where to look first, whether to shoot them or swing the torch. In the end, he opted to wait, his heart pounding — most of them were still held back by the circles of flame, but that wouldn't last long.

There were so many of them now, so many! It was Beekman's Diner all over again — they were all staring at him, reaching out for him, gasping, moaning, *lusting* for him, for his flesh. And creeping ever nearer.

In the truck, Tom tried to put the key into the ignition, but his hand was shaking so badly he kept missing. The first thing still hadn't regained its feet, but the second was right there — inches away! — pawing at the window. Tom looked over at it; he couldn't help himself. He saw the clammy, discolored skin; the horrible, infected-looking gash along the left side of its jaw near its mouth — hell, as far as he knew, that wound is what killed it, only to bring it back.

Tom looked away, sickened. And finally drove the key home.

In the house by the open cellar, Judy heard the struggles, the ghastly ululations through the open front door, and when she heard the truck's engine turn over and start, she made her decision in the blink of an eye.

"I'm going with him."

And then she was running across the room toward the front door.

Mister Cooper heard her, saw her coming, and tried to block her way. "Get back in the cellar!" he ordered, grabbing at her arms.

"No!" she cried.

"It's too late!"

And he was right, but not in the way he thought. It *was* too late, because her mind was made up and there was no way in hell she was letting Tommy leave without her!

Outside, Ben heard the struggle over the rumble of the truck. He whirled about, expecting to find that one of the creatures had somehow made it onto the porch and was trying to get into the house. Instead, he was surprised to see the girl, Judy, shoving her way past Cooper and running into the yard.

Tom caught the movement from the corner of his eye and looked through the windshield. His jaw dropped in horror twice over:

First, because *Judy* was outside, skidding to a halt in front of the truck as she spotted the things that were trying to get at him.

Second, because at that moment, Cooper slammed the front door shut.

Judy heard it, looked behind her, then back to Tom. She was frozen, her bravado from a moment before evaporating as the reality of what she was doing — had already done — sank in.

Tom gaped at her a second longer, then twisted back toward the driver's window, slapping his palm against it, anything to keep the creatures' attention on *him*, to keep them from noticing his Judy standing out there, exposed.

Ben, bless him, broke the spell. He shouted at her, "Well if you're coming, *come on!*"

Judy hurried around to the passenger side.

Ben set the torch down in the grass, grasped the rifle with both hands. "Get in!" he snapped.

He wouldn't get any argument from her! Judy opened the door and leaped into the truck.

Ben took aim and fired at one of the things as it drew closer. The slug pounded into its chest and out through its back — it stumbled a moment, its momentum halted ... and then it was shambling forward once more.

Ben thought frantically. The only injuries that seemed to put them down for good was damage to the head, to the *brain*. But he was a high school teacher, damn it — he knew his way around a gun from childhood hunting with his father, but he was a far cry from being a marksman.

Rather than waste more ammo from this distance (not that the distance was all that great by now), Ben stooped and reclaimed his torch. Whatever harm they could or could not withstand, they were *afraid* of fire, and that was his one solid advantage. He waved the torch toward one, then another.

They slowed, but did not stop.

More of them had reached Tom's side of the truck — for an unsettling, surreal moment, he found himself staring at a glistening wedding ring, still in place on its bloated, blue finger.

If they waited much longer, they would be overwhelmed. They had to get moving!

Tom put the truck into gear.

Ben heard the shift in the motor and took the hint. Tossing the rifle ahead of him, still brandishing the torch, he climbed over the side and into the bed of the truck.

As if sensing their prey were about to escape, the

things — the *dead* — swarmed forward as fast as their bungling feet would carry them.

Having locked the front door, Harry Cooper rushed over to one of the windows. He crouched, peering through the openings between two nailed slats, desperate to follow what was happening outside.

Ben slipped, nearly losing his footing as the truck lurched. The dead were too damned close; Tom needed to get the truck moving, to gain some speed before he could just knock them out of the way.

Ben tried to help, thrusting the torch in every direction. One of them got too close, and Ben shoved the torch against its belly. Its dirty evening jacket caught fire and it stumbled away, slapping at the licking flames, the concept of Stop-Drop-and-Roll beyond its limited comprehension.

But there were plenty of others to take its place.

Cooper switched from gap to gap, trying to see better. He wanted to scream! Why in the world weren't they moving yet?!

As if Cooper's frustration lent much-needed inertia to the truck, Tom finally got it rolling backward. He didn't run any of them over, but he knocked them down and out of the way. Wheezing and gasping, several tried to hold on to the truck, unwilling to give them up — Ben leaned over the cabin and thrust the torch against hands, into faces.

The dead fell back, and the truck was clear. Tom shoved it into a forward gear, and they were on their way!

The truck pulled around the house, out of sight from Cooper's vantage point. Cooper hesitated — he knew he should probably stay next to the front door, since they would be coming back with those things hot on their heels ... but in the end, he couldn't contain himself. He dashed toward the back of the house.

As Tom drove around to the gas pump by the barn,

they encountered more of the dead coming in from the back fields. He gripped the steering wheel tight, knowing their venture had *better* work now, because all this racket was drawing more of them in than ever. He was forced to slow down as some of them bounced off the fenders, only to have others clamber along the sides. Ben held steady in the back, waving the torch every which way.

Tom wanted to gun the engine and get the hell away from this new group, but just then the engine coughed once, reminding him that they were too low on fuel for any jackrabbit stunts. Instead, he ground his teeth, reached over to hold Judy's hand, and pressed on in low gear.

Cooper ran into the kitchen, looked around, and located the window that would best serve him. He shoved the drapes aside, leaning back and forth until he spotted them near the barn. Yes, they had pulled away from the rest of those things and were almost to the pump. They were going to make it!

Tom eased the old Chevy around in an arc toward their destination. A glance through the side mirror revealed over a dozen of the dead zeroing in on them, but they were far enough away that they should have plenty of time to fill the tank, so long as they *hurried*.

Leaving the engine running, Tom leaped from the cabin and sprinted for the pump. Ben jumped down from the bed, the torch and rifle in each hand. As Tom shoved the key into the rusty padlock on the pump handle, Ben set the torch down on the ground where he could grab it again at a moment's notice, and held the rifle at ready. But when he turned, he saw Tom still fumbling with the lock.

"Come on!" he urged.

Frustrated and terrified, Tom told him, "This key won't work!"

Ben never wavered. He took Tom by the arm and

pulled him away from the pump. "Watch out."

He didn't have to tell Tom twice. The young man backed away as Ben aimed the rifle.

At near point-blank range, Ben blew the lock to smithereens. The blast echoed through the night, and would undoubtedly bring more of the dead shambling toward them, but Tom knew they would be long gone by then. They just had to *hurry*!

It was the second time Tom had told himself as much. And it was his undoing.

He raced to the pump, tossed aside the stray remains of the padlock, seized the handle in a firm grip and spun around toward the truck. Unfortunately, that firm grip squeezed the pump lever halfway down, and gasoline sprayed and splashed everywhere — through the air, all over the side of the truck, and onto the ground ...

... where Ben had laid the burning table leg.

"Watch the torch!" Ben cried, diving for it.

Too late. Ben dragged it away, but not before the gasoline caught. In the blink of an eye, the back-right half of the truck was covered in fire!

In the kitchen, Cooper had been straining to see what was happening out there in the dark, but when flames raced up the side of the truck, he saw it just fine. His heart shot up into his throat and his bowels washed over cold as he watched his daughter's best chance for rescue burning in the night. His pulse raced and his head pounded.

Those bastard ... those clumsy, stupid *bastards!*

This time, Ben had no idea what to do. The flames were as spread out as those created by the Molotov cocktails, but these were burning hotter and spreading faster. Too much to snuff out by kicking dirt on it, not in the little time they had before the dead caught up to the them.

What should he do? What should he *do*?!

Tom, so flustered that he wasn't fully conscious of his own mistake, tried to sneak in around the side, tried to get the nozzle into the waiting gas tank, but it was pointless — the fire was too intense.

Tom was more panicked than ever, but what made it worse was that he didn't *know* that he was panicking. He shouted, "We gotta get away from the pump!" and ran back around toward the driver's side of the truck.

Unfortunately, Ben wasn't listening. He had remembered a dirty old blanket in the bed of the truck, dragged it out and toward the fire. He was reluctant to put down the gun since he would need it again at any time, so he tossed the blanket down and moved it around with his foot. If they could just get it smothered fast enough ...

In a classic case of the right hand not knowing what the left hand was doing, Tom jumped in behind the steering wheel. He got the truck into gear and told Judy, "Hang on!"

She nodded, trusting Tom to do the right thing.

Ben looked up to see the truck pulling away, the back-right tire burning and throwing the flames further onto the underside of the vehicle.

"*Tom!*" he cried. "Tom, you're crazy— *Get out of the truck!*"

Tom heard Ben shouting, but he couldn't make out what he was saying, nor would it have made any difference if he could. All he could think was to get the burning truck away from the gas pumps, away from the pumps, *away* from the *pumps*!

Cooper couldn't fathom what was happening out there. The truck was driving away, but it was clearly on fire and could not have had time to fill up on fuel. And it was so dark and it looked like more of those things were appearing in the field now and ...

There *were* more dead walking in the field — some of them were advancing on the truck, others were wandering toward the house, but a number of them were headed straight for Ben. He was still trying to put out the ground fire before it could reach the pump, but while he had it somewhat contained, he also had more than a few minor burns to show for it. He kept the gun close, knowing that he would need to provide cover for Tom and Judy when they finally got it through their heads to abandon the lost truck.

A fair distance away, Tom at last reached that very conclusion. He jammed the truck into Park and threw his door open.

"Let's get outta here!" he yelled over his shoulder.

But when he turned around, Judy wasn't following him. She sat on the passenger side of the seat, her hair in disarray and her eyes wild, gaping at him.

"Come on," he cried, "come on!"

She struggled, but still wasn't moving. Before he could ask, she panted, "My jacket's caught!"

Tom leaped back into the truck, threw himself across the seat. Her denim jacket had indeed gotten caught in the passenger door, but when he tried to open it he learned why she had not done that simple act — the fire had spread to the door, and the handle was searing hot.

No time! He grabbed the door handle again, clenching his teeth against the pain, he had to do it, there was no time, no time!

No time.

Boom!

At the house, Cooper cried out and shielded his eyes. The window rattled so hard, he thought it might burst inward and shower him with glass.

Even though Ben was outside and much closer to the explosion, he found himself unable to look away. So little gas had remained in the tank, he couldn't believe it could erupt into such a fierce conflagration, but it had. Black smoke billowed into the sky and flames engulfed the truck cabin ...

... with Tom and Judy still inside.

With everything he had seen since Beekman's, Ben didn't think he could be shocked anymore tonight, if ever again. But as he gazed upon the fiery deaths of those two sweet kids, he felt numb all over.

Cooper panted, near hyperventilating as the truck burned. Their one chance, their *one fucking chance*! Seething in anger and frustration and close to tears, he closed the drapes and backed away from the kitchen window.

Ben took a step forward, thinking that maybe — *maybe*— Tom or Judy might still be alive and needed help ... but no, it was the gas station explosion all over again, and in more ways than one.

When he looked around, the dead were already losing interest in the truck and were fixating on *him*.

Where in the hell were they all coming from? It was as though they were spawning right out here in the field. At Beekman's, from the gowns and uniforms, he had concluded that most of them had spread out from the county hospital. But now they appeared to come from all walks of life.

Walks of "life," huh? Good one, Ben.

He bit his tongue hard to kill the laughter that threatened to bubble up from the back of his throat. Too treacherous — if he gave in to that whim, he could easily end up as lost and helpless as Barbra, if not downright deranged.

Ben lifted the rifle, took aim, and fired at the closest one. It was again a heart-shot, and would have dropped any living man in his tracks. But the dead man just stopped, tipped over backward almost to the point of falling on his ass, then rocked forward and continued moving toward Ben.

Ben considered going for the head-shot, but the same inner debate zipped through his mind in about two seconds — he just wasn't a sharpshooter, and didn't want to waste ammo.

So once more, he scooped up his torch.

But though they still cringed and flinched, the dead weren't as intimidated by his portable little flame — not after the brilliance of the burning truck. He waved the torch in a wide arc and the dead recoiled, but they wouldn't give any ground.

Ben swallowed, his dry tongue making a clicking sound against the sandpaper that was the roof of his mouth, and stepped closer to them.

His gamble paid off. When he started actually *touching* them with the flames, when sparks sizzled from their clothing and singed their skin, they finally backed off just enough to let him squeeze through the front ranks.

But he was far from home-free. Everywhere he looked, from every direction, the living dead were closing in.

Holding his torch before him, Ben zigged and zagged back toward the house, relying on their timidity of the fire and his own superior dexterity to get him through. They couldn't see in the dark any better than he could, so as he slipped deeper into the night, his torch paled in contrast and some of them lost their focus, started wandering aimlessly once more.

But there were still plenty more that were willing to

make the extra effort to devour him.

Ben ran faster.

Finally, he gained enough lead and clearance to make a dash straight for the house. For the moment, none of them were near the front door, but he knew that wouldn't last long. He needed to get his ass inside, right now!

Harry Cooper was about to step through the cellar door when he was startled — *stunned*, really — to hear Ben call from outside, "Let me in!" There had been so many of those things out there, how could the man have possibly made it back to the house?

Ben slammed into the front door, expecting Cooper to have opened it already. All it did was jar his shoulder as he bounced off the unyielding barrier.

"Let me in!" he yelled again. Looking behind him, he saw another wave of the dead advancing upon the house, and his torch seemed a pitiful shield. This time he hit the door with his fist. "Cooper!"

Cooper lingered in the cellar doorway, torn. He stepped further into the stairwell, then froze again. He knew the best thing to do, the *right* thing to do, would be to shut the door and join his family and Barbra below. Ben had been nothing but trouble, and now that Tom and Judy were gone, the food they had collected would last that much longer.

But ...

Outside, Ben shouted, "*Cooper!*" once more. Then the gasps and wheezing pulled his attention back to the front yard. The torch was now in danger of burning out altogether — Ben thrust forward, throwing it at the dead. They would be on him in seconds!

Cooper had found it much easier to dehumanize Barbra and Ben when they had been nothing but noisemakers from overhead, screams and shouts that meant very little to him with no face to associate with them. Now, regardless of how he felt about the arrogant prick, he *knew* Ben, had argued with him and worked with him, to a point.

This time, Cooper took a step out of the cellar, *toward* the front door. But once again, he froze with indecision. What should he do?!

Ben made the decision for him.

Hauling back, Ben kicked the door with everything he had. The door jam gave way, and as wood splintered inward ahead of the swinging door, he stumbled forward with so much momentum, he almost took a face dive right onto the rug.

The sudden noise startled Cooper into retreating back into the cellar stairwell. When he realized who it was and what had happened, he stopped short of closing the door.

But the look Ben gave him made him almost wish he had. Ben's fierce gaze bore straight into his soul, and Cooper knew that there would be hell to pay if he didn't retreat right now. But he was afraid to budge an inch — from the heat in Ben's eyes, he considered himself lucky that Ben didn't shoot him on the spot!

Ben indulged himself in that one-second glare at Cooper, then turned and slammed the front door shut. But the problem was, he had just *broken* through the door to get inside — the doorknob would no longer catch, let alone lock. Setting the rifle aside, Ben grabbed the nearby loose door they had removed for lumber and shoved it crossways against the front door.

Once he was out of Ben's sights, Cooper found he could move again. This was his chance — while Ben was wasting time, he could close and barricade the cellar. He had warned them all along, he had *warned* them, but no, they wouldn't listen to him!

All that was well and good, but if he had felt conflicted upon hearing Ben's voice calling to him, he discovered he simply could not turn away now that Ben was inside and struggling to keep those things at bay.

He wanted to, he wanted to turn away and leave the bastard to his just punishment, but when he imagined the look in Helen's eyes — or, God forbid, *Karen's* once she got better — he ... he just couldn't do it.

So, much to his own surprise, Harry Cooper found himself running across the room and throwing his weight against the barrier alongside Ben, bracing it with everything he had as the dead pushed from the other side.

Together, they pressed the barricade flat enough for Ben to start hammering it into place. Ben hustled back and forth, pounding the barricade on one side then the other, shoving Cooper aside as he worked, sending the smaller man rushing to and fro, holding and pushing and bracing wherever he was needed. It probably took no more than a couple of minutes, but for the two sweating, panting men, it felt more like an hour.

When they had nearly finished the job, when the door was no longer shuddering from the dead's assault, Ben looked over at Cooper. The man was fidgeting and licking his dry lips, reluctant to meet Ben's gaze. His eyes pleaded with Ben for understanding, for mercy. *See?* those beady eyes seemed to say. *I helped you re-blockade the front door! We're even now, right?*

An anger — no, a *rage* — built within Ben like nothing he had ever before experienced. This glib, belligerent little man had caused trouble from the moment Ben had laid eyes on him, countermining and subverting at every turn. He had been willing to let Barbra fend for herself, had let Ben and then Tom do all the work on securing the house ... and then, when Ben and Tom and

Judy had risked their lives to save *his daughter* as much as themselves, the motherfucker had been willing to leave Ben outside as one more feast for the living dead.

A small, still-rational part of Ben's mind knew that this was pointless, that it would accomplish nothing and it certainly would not bring Tom or Judy back. But for now, that part was in recession; for now, the *rage* was in charge, and Ben meant to indulge it.

Dropping the hammer lest he be tempted to use it, Ben clenched his teeth and his fist — his left fist, where he wore his bulky class ring. He lashed out, catching Cooper square in the mouth. Cooper crumpled away and Ben seized him by the front of his shirt, refusing to let him fall until he had delivered an equally powerful right cross.

Cooper went down onto his hands and knees, crawling away from Ben toward the study. When he reached the doorframe, he had just managed to climb up to his feet, like a drunk getting his second wind, when Ben delivered another punch to the face. Cooper dropped again, catching and then trying to climb up onto an armchair — a nonsensical move, but then, Cooper's thinking wasn't very clear at the moment.

Ben decided to stop there, that the man had had enough ... so he was surprised to find himself grabbing the man by the back of his disheveled shirt, pulling him onto his feet once again, and delivering the most devastating blow yet — a roundhouse punch to Cooper's bobbing chin.

Cooper went down hard this time, sprawling against another chair and showing no intention of getting back to his feet. Ben descended upon him once more, and wondered if his hands would continue to act on their own and rain more blows upon the helpless prick.

But no, he settled for grabbing Cooper in a harsh grip and hauling him up into the chair. Which was a good thing, because if the beating had continued, he might have killed the man.

Bending over Cooper, looming over him, he spat, "I outta *drag* you out there and *feed* you to those things!"

Ben shoved away from Cooper in disgust.

Cooper said nothing in return, offered no defense; he remained collapsed where he was, blood running from his nose and mouth, his eyes wide and unfocused and woeful. He lay there whimpering under his breath as Ben stormed out of the room, his mind a whirlwind of hateful thoughts (and self-loathing guilt) ...

Out in the field, the dead drew closer to the truck as the flames ran their course. Their moaning swelled in pitch alongside their excitement, until the night slithered and crept with a cacophony of their hellish delight.

Ben and Cooper had both seen the truck explode. Ben and Cooper both believed that Tom and Judy had died in the flames.

Ignorance, as they say, was bliss.

The truck's gas tank had indeed been nearly empty, and in the dark night, the flames created more light than heat. The concussive force behind the eruption had knocked the young lovers into a daze, the flames stealing all the oxygen and leaving them unable to voice their screams, their agony.

Now they lay together in a stupor, third-degree burns covering their bodies, conscious thought blessedly elusive through their fog of anguish. They clung to life by the thinnest of threads ... but however frail, that thread was still intact.

Tom and Judy were still alive.

Which is what drew the dead to them.

They crawled over the truck like maggots over putrid meat, scrambling through the open driver's door and the melted windshield. Their clawing hands sank and ripped into tender flesh, rending and ripping it to shreds while the victims trembled, incapable of reacting in any useful way.

It was an appalling way to die, but it ended Tom and Judy's suffering.

When little remained of the young couple, the dead spread out with their ghastly bounty, many of them sinking to their knees beneath the bright moon as it broke through the clouds. Those with solid chunks of meat — a thigh, a pectoral, a heart — sat quietly and feasted. Others who had ended up with intestines and other loose matter thrashed and fought over their pith; one might have called it "playing with their food," had they not been so mindless. Arms and legs, hands and feet were treated like legs of chicken, the soft gristle torn and plucked from bones and tendons in familiar fashion.

For the time being, the dead were satisfied.

Ben turned away from the window where he had watched the dead consuming the remains of Tom and Judy. At first it had been too dark, the shadows a vague orgy of furtive movement ... but when the moon came out, he saw what was happening all too clearly.

He gagged, his guts clenching, his throat tightening. A cold, acrid sweat broke out on his forehead, across the back of his neck. He was going to lose it, he knew he was ...

Then the urge passed, though the memory of what he had just seen remained painfully fresh and threatened to lift his gorge again at a moment's notice.

Ben lowered himself into a wooden dining chair. He sat, just sat and focused on breathing, slow and even. He gripped the rifle in both hands, using it not as a weapon but to help himself feel more grounded.

Across the room, Cooper sat nursing the wounds Ben

had delivered upon him, a wet cloth held against his sore, swollen left cheek. Behind him, his wife Helen appeared at the top of the cellar stairs, her stride shaky and tenuous. Ben barely glanced at her, but he could see that she was exhausted.

She stopped in the doorway, rubbing both temples against a headache. Her gaze flickered to Harry on the chair and Barbra back on the sofa, and asked, "Isn't it three o'clock yet ...?" She glanced back down the stairs, toward where her little girl rested, then registered that no one had answered her. She parked herself just outside the doorway and said with more force, "There's supposed to be another broadcast at three o'clock."

"Ten minutes ..." was Cooper's muttered reply.

"Oh?" Barbra perked up. "Only ten more minutes? We don't have very long to wait. We can leave." When no one commented, she continued, "Well, we better leave soon. It's ten minutes to three."

Ben had no idea what was going on in her head at this point, but he didn't like that all of them — himself included — seemed to be catching her lost, disjointed neurosis. They had lost Tom and Judy; they would not lose anyone else. Not if *he* had anything to say about it, goddamn it!

Shaking himself into motion, Ben checked the rifle's ammunition, then dragged the box of bullets closer and began reloading. As he worked, he asked the Coopers, "Do you know anything about this area at all? I mean, *is* Willard the nearest town?"

Helen looked over at him. She thought about it for a moment, hugged herself tighter. "I don't know ..." Then she sighed and stood straighter, peeking down the cellar stairs again, toward Karen. "We were ... just trying to get to a motel before dark."

Ben nodded. "You say those things turned your car

over. You think we can get it back on its wheels and drive it?" Then the important question. "Where is it?"

Helen answered, her voice sounding more tired than ever, "Seems like it was pretty far away ... seems like we ran ..."

Then Cooper spoke up, sounding irritated and petulant. "Forgot it. It's at least a mile."

"Johnny has the keys," Barbra sing-songed from the sofa.

Cooper tossed over his shoulder at his wife, "You gonna carry that child a *mile*? Through that army of *things* out there?"

Ben stated, "I can carry the kid."

Cooper's eyes shot daggers at him from across the room, but the little man said nothing.

Ben ignored him, asking Helen, "What's wrong with her? How'd she get hurt?"

"One of those things grabbed her—" she answered.

Cooper cut in, his eyes averted, "Bit her on the arm."

Shit, Ben thought. Tom had mentioned that the girl was hurt, but Ben had yet to see her with his own eyes, hadn't thought to ask exactly *how* she had been injured.

Helen noticed his expression. "What's wrong?"

"Who knows *what* kind of disease those things carry?"

Helen just stared at him — the same thought had been on her mind, of course, since the television stressed how important it was to get the wounded medical treatment.

"Is she conscious?" Ben asked.

"Barely."

Cooper piped up again. "She can't walk, she's too weak."

Ben looked away, fighting the urge to spring across the room and beat the rest of that obstinance out of the man. The frustrating thing was, if the girl was sick with something, Cooper was probably right — Ben had gotten back to the house by the skin of his teeth; he couldn't imagine carrying a child through a mile of that.

But that didn't mean he had to like it, so he yelled, "Well, *one* of us could try to get to the car!"

Cooper sneered, "You gonna turn it over by *yourself?*"

"You can't start the car," Barbra scolded them, "Johnny has the *keys.*"

That's when Ben set aside his irritation with Cooper long enough to consider what Barbra was saying. Maybe she wasn't just blabbering after all.

Crossing to her, he knelt down and asked, "*You* have a car?"

Even Cooper looked interested in the answer, but Barbra didn't say anything, just looked at Ben with that same drunken expression.

"*Where?*" Ben stressed. "Where is it?"

Barbra shook her head and spoke in that same sing-song voice, as though she were addressing a silly child. "You won't be able to start it."

Ben was losing his patience. "Yeah, yeah, I know, but where *is* it?"

But before she could answer, they were all startled by a sudden loud moan from outside the front door.

The dead had been quieter than usual while they were having their way with Tom and Judy's remains. But now that the flesh was dwindling, they were no longer satisfied, but revitalized, aroused with the desire for more. They descended upon the house like sharks drawn to blood, vocalizing their need louder than before.

They wanted more ... more ... and what they wanted was inside that house.

Ben rushed to the window, saw them coming. He gripped one of the boards tight, grinding his teeth in fear and frustration. But what could he do? At a loss, he turned around and flipped on the television — maybe the next broadcast would provide something useful for a change.

Cooper had also hurried to the window, but unlike Ben, he remained ... and was christened with his own front-row presentation of what they faced. It was one thing to hear it on the television; it was something else to see it with his own eyes.

"Good Lord ..." he whispered.

The dead were not completely out of sustenance just yet. As a group, they had moved closer to the house, to the source of more ... but as individuals, they continued to feast upon the remnants of Tom and Judy. A hand here, a foot there, other parts which Cooper could not recognize, and was glad for that.

It was true. The dead were *eating* the living.

The anchorman was talking on the television now, and Cooper forced himself to back away from the window and try to pay attention. He strode over to sit near his wife, while Ben hunkered down almost directly in front of the television set.

"*... being monitored closely by scientists and all the radiation detection stations,*" the anchorman was saying. "*At this hour, they report the level of the mysterious radiation continues to increase steadily. So long as this situation remains, government spokesmen warn that dead bodies will continue to be transformed into the flesh-eating ghouls.*"

Cooper had just gotten settled when his agitation forced him back to his feet. The movement caught Ben's attention — the high-and-mighty bastard glanced over his shoulder at him, gripping that rifle of his to send a message.

He wouldn't be so goddamn tough, Cooper groused, *without that gun.* But he knew to keep that opinion to himself, so he said nothing. Instead, he crossed the room again, peered out through the window for a brief moment, then turned away once more in repulsion.

"*All persons who die during this crisis,*" the anchorman continued, "*from whatever cause, will come back to life — to seek human victims — unless their bodies are first disposed of by cremation.*"

The anchorman paused, then spoke with renewed energy.

"*Our news cameras have just returned from covering such a search-and-destroy operation against the ghouls, this one conducted by Sheriff Conan McClelland in Butler County, Pennsylvania. So now let's go to that film report...*"

The image cut away to an exterior which could have been shot down the road, so far as Ben could tell — the trees and large, grassy lawns looked familiar enough. A rural house stood in the background, a police car waited in the foreground, and in the middle a crowd of men, all carrying guns.

"*All law enforcement agencies,*" the anchorman narrated, "*and the military have been organized to search out and destroy the marauding ghouls.*"

As the image switched to a closeup of even more men, mostly civilians but all still armed, something nagged at Ben, itching at the back of his mind that something wasn't right. But he couldn't place what it was at first, so he continued listening.

"*Survival Command Center at the Pentagon has disclosed that a ghoul can be* killed *by a shot in the head, or a heavy blow to the skull.*"

For the first time in hours, Ben brightened, if only for a moment. He had been right!

"*Officials are quoted as explaining that since the*

brain of a ghoul has been activated by the radiation, the plan is: Kill the brain, and you kill the ghoul."

The sound quality changed as they switched to the recording from the field. Police officers in uniform exchanged comments with others who were not, while a reporter waited for a moment to jump in with his questions.

Ben tuned that out for a moment — two things were bothering him now, but as if in compliment of each other, he figured out what they each were.

The first, the one that had bugged him from the moment they had switched to the film footage, was the *time of day* in which it was shot — broad daylight. When he had noticed the daylight during the earlier interview with the military officer and his two companions, Ben had presumed that it had been filmed somewhere on the west coast, where the sun might not have set yet. But this footage, which the anchorman claimed had "just" returned, looked like mid-afternoon, whereas it was now nighttime across the entire nation.

They're misleading us, he thought. *They're trying to prevent further panic at best, or boldface-lying to us at worst. This has been going on longer than they're willing to admit.*

The second thing was this bit about mysterious radiation having "activated" the brains of the dead; the notion had made him skeptical earlier, and it did so again. He believed the part about destroying the brain — he'd come to that conclusion on his own, seen the evidence with his own eyes — but as for "mysterious radiation" being the cause, he just didn't buy it. Again, he was no expert, but to his knowledge irradiating the brain would, if anything, be a possible *solution* to the problem; the accelerated particles would tear the awakened synapses apart, break down the cells ...

The real problem is, he realized, *that they don't have a* clue *why this is happening or what is causing it. But this must be their best working theory, so they're presenting it as fact.*

Damn. This situation wouldn't be going away anytime soon.

On the television, the reporter finally got in close enough to try for an interview, *"Chief? Chief McClelland, how's everything going?"*

The man turned around, and Ben was surprised to learn that he wasn't a conscripted civilian — he seemed a little too rough around the edges to be a competent police officer. He carried a rifle on one shoulder and wore a large bandoleer across his girthy chest. He also wore a Fedora-style hat, and tucked into the hatband were what appeared to be three wrapped cigars, as if the man intended to pass them around to celebrate a newborn.

"Ah, things aren't goin' too bad," the Chief replied. *"Men are takin' it pretty good."* He looked over the reporter's shoulder and shouted, *"You wanna get on the other side of the road over there!"*

"Chief," the reporter asked, bringing his attention back around, *"do you think we'll be able to defeat these things?"*

"Well we killed nineteen of 'em today right in this area. Those last three we caught tryin' ta claw their way into an abandoned shed, they musta thought somebody was in there. There wadn't, though. We heard 'em makin' all kinda noise, we came over an' beat 'em off, blasted 'em down."

From off camera, someone shouted something Ben couldn't understand, and the Chief answered, *"Yeah, okay!"*

Desperate to hold onto this interview, the reporter

jumped in, *"Chief, uh ... if I were surrounded by six or eight of these things, would I stand a chance with them?"*

"Well there's no problem. If you had a gun, shoot 'em in the head, that's a sure way ta kill 'em. If you don't, get yourself a club or a torch — beat 'em or burn 'em, they go up pretty easy."

"Chief McClelland, how long do you think it will take you until you get the situation under control?"

"Well that's pretty hard ta say, we don't know how many of 'em there are. We know when we find 'em, we can kill 'em."

"Are they slow-moving, Chief?"

"Yeah, they're dead, they're ..." the man paused, as if considering something profound, then delivered, *"... all messed up."*

Ben shook his head. *"All messed up?"* What a callous son of a bitch. How a backwards redneck like that made Chief of Police is just ludicrous, it's ...

He stopped himself. Whether his evaluation of the chief were accurate or not, this attitude was unlike him ... as unlike him as those extra blows he had delivered onto Cooper.

Ben needed to watch himself. He didn't like the effect Cooper was having on him — these ugly thoughts were brought on by dealing with Cooper as much as with the dead people, and the obnoxious little man wasn't worth it.

"Well, uh," the reporter asked, *"in time ... would you say you ought to be able to wrap this up in twenty-four hours?"*

"Well ..." McClelland considered, *"... we don't really know. We know we'll be into it mosta the night, probly into the early morning. We're workin' our way toward Willard, an we'll team up with the National Guard over there, an then we'll be able ta getta more definite view."*

Ben noted the reference to Willard. So this *was* recorded in the local area, which meant from the sunlight that this was shot many hours ago, before the attack on Beekman's had even occurred.

"Thank you very much, Chief McClelland."

The chief nodded and faded back.

The reporter addressed the camera directly, *"This is Bill Cardille, WIC TV-11 news."*

The view switched back to the studio, and the anchorman said, *"Thank you, Bill, for that report."*

Ben glanced over his shoulder at the others. Were they noticing the discontinuity between the report and the way it was being presented as though it were "current"? Should he point it out? What would that accomplish? Barbra was too out of it, Helen was too exhausted, and he couldn't care less about Cooper.

Besides, it didn't really change their situation, did it?

"Official spokesmen decline to speculate," the anchorman was saying, *"just how long it may take to kill off all the flesh-eaters. So long as the heavy ra—"*

And then their situation changed.

The television fell silent as the room plunged into darkness. The quartet tensed, looking up as if they might bring the lights back on by force of will.

Ben stood. Maybe — *maybe* — this was just a God-awful coincidence. "Is the fuse box in the cellar?"

"I don't know ..." Cooper said, his voice uneven and tentative. "I ..."

Harry Cooper hated to show his fear, especially to the son of a bitch who'd had the nerve to lay hands on him. But the fact was that the sudden darkness disturbed him even more than seeing those things outside eating what was left of Tom and Judy. He felt so ... damned ... *helpless!*

Ben strode past him toward the cellar, then

disappeared from what little light there was into total blackness as he descended the stairs, probably looking for the stupid fuse box.

But Harry knew better. He could feel it. "It ... it isn't the fuse," he whispered. "The power lines are down."

Yes, that was it. Those things weren't as stupid as they looked — they'd cut the power! And here he stood, helpless. If he couldn't even defend himself against Ben ...

No, this was intolerable, and he had to do something about it.

Turning, he moved over to his wife where she sat on the arm of the sofa. Keeping his voice low, he said, "Helen ... I have to get that *gun*."

His eyes were adjusting to the gloom, picking up on what little light was leaking through the boarded windows, but Helen's face was still a phantom before him. But even though he couldn't see her, he heard her scoff. And when she answered, the ice, the disgust, in her voice was unmistakable. "Haven't you had *enough*?"

"Wha—?" Harry stammered, flabbergasted by her attitude. She was his wife, goddamn it! "Two people are dead already on account of that guy. Take a look out that window. We can't—"

Then Ben reappeared, and Harry shut his mouth in a hurry. He looked away, trembling as much in frustration as in fear, as Ben strode past him.

If only those things had gotten the bastard, *he* would be in charge!

Outside, one of the dead stared down at the ground. He was nearer to the house than some of the others, and he wasn't looking at any of the small remaining fires or pieces of Tom or Judy or even a fieldmouse. He was looking at a rock, a large jagged stone bigger than his gashed hand.

Something about that rock was tickling at what little remained of the dead man's mind. Some association, some use *perhaps?*

If Ben or Cooper had observed this behavior, they would likely have found it confusing, but Barbra *might have been able to explain it to them — it was a reaction she had seen before, albeit at a much faster, more instinctive pace.*

And then the dead man had it. Bending slowly, his stiff muscles and grinding bones creaking and popping, he reached down and picked up the rock. He hefted it once, twice, then moved toward the house, the rock held ready.

His example triggered an instant reaction in one of the others. He, too, bent over, in his case near the still-smoldering chair Ben had pushed outside hours earlier. He grabbed the end of Ben's first makeshift torch and, dragging the discarded table leg behind him, he shambled up onto the front porch. As he approached the front door, moving more on instinct than actual thought, he heaved the table leg up so that he could close both bluish hands around it ...

... then swung it around and slammed it against the front door.

In the house, it all seemed to start happening at once. A loud, sharp *thunk* came from the front door, but before Ben could do much more than turn his head toward the sound, another bang came from further down the porch, and then another on the heels of that. Far too fast and too far apart to be coming from the same creature. Nothing had been happening a moment ago, and now it sounded as though a whole group of them had figured out how to use objects as tools, as *weapons*.

Ben's assumption wasn't far off. As if the first dead man's picking up the rock had triggered an inexplicable

*burst of evolution — an insidious "Ah-ha!" moment —
many of the dead grabbed rocks and branches and
whatever they could find close at hand and began
assaulting the house in earnest. They weren't even sure
why they were doing it, not exactly, but they knew that
prey was inside, and this suddenly struck them as the right
thing to do to get at what they wanted.*

The din grew at a frightening rate. They all looked
around, speechless, unsure what to do — even Barbra
absorbed that some critical conversion had taken place, and
though she said nothing to the others, she *did*, in fact, think
back to that first dead man's picking up the rock and
breaking through Johnny's car window.

Barbra's recollection was almost prophetic — right on
its heels, the dead man who had started the current ruckus
by picking up the rock got close enough to a window to
pitch his burden through the glass. The stone not only
shattered the bottom window panes, it knocked some of
Ben's handiwork askew, jarring the lumber loose on its
nails.

Ben raced forward, holding the rifle crossways against
the planks of wood as the thing outside followed up on its
assault. Another joined it, and Ben struggled to keep the
barricade in place.

Harry Cooper watched from across the room, licking
his lips in excitement in spite of his fear. If the bastard
happened to lose his grip, to *drop* that gun ...

Helen Cooper, on the other hand, was thinking of
survival in a different light. She had leaned against the
front door, to support the barricade there, but the pounding
kicked up a notch, and the whole structure began to tremble
and shake. Gasping, she turned toward it, trying to place
her hands in the best positions possible, to brace the door
wherever she could. She didn't know exactly *why* Ben had

to break the lock to get back into the house earlier, but she suspected Harry had something to do with it, and now she cursed her husband for his shortsightedness!

Ben could see the dead people staring at him through the gaps in the barricade. All through the evening, they had rarely seemed aware of his looking out through the windows, but they were now. Their eyes widened and their teeth gnashed as they practically drooled over the sight of him. It reminded him of a wasp he'd seen outside his bedroom window as a child — young Ben had placed his hand against the glass where the insect was bumping around, and it kept attacking the pane on the other side of his fingers, trying to sting him, repeatedly, even though he was beyond its reach.

The big difference here was, Ben wasn't sure how much longer he would *remain* beyond the dead's reach. Their hands snaked through the broken panes, heedless of the jagged glass which tore deep trenches into their graying flesh. Ben twisted away from those grasping hands while still trying to brace the barricade as best he could — it was a dance he would not be able to keep up for much longer.

Helen saw his dilemma from her own struggle at the front door, but she could do nothing to help him without abandoning her post. She sympathized with his plight — God, if one of those things laid a hand on her ...

Where the *hell* was *HARRY*?!

She glanced over her shoulder to see her idiot husband just standing there across the room. What was wrong with him?! Couldn't he see they needed *help*?!

Ben was wondering the same thing. He twisted around and yelled, "Get over here, man!"

Cooper *still* hesitated.

"Come *on*!" Ben bellowed. And the distraction cost him.

Too many hands — Ben hadn't heard it, but the upper panes must have broken or been ripped loose, too, because now the dead were reaching through the boards at all points of the window. One of the diagonal boards bulged outward in spite of his weight and the nails, and threatened to tear loose altogether. He couldn't manage this with only one free hand anymore and he couldn't shoot at them under these circumstances, so he dropped the rifle to the floor beside him.

Harry's eyes lit up when the gun tumbled to the rug. Yes! But ... could he get to it without Ben realizing what he was up to? He had no desire for another beating.

Helen saw it happen, too, and turned her back to the door once again, watching her husband. Were his priorities so distorted? God knew Harry was a flawed man and husband, but was he *that* blind?

Harry watched Ben carefully, watched him in his pointless struggle as *exactly* what he had predicted happened before their eyes — all these flimsy boards would never keep those things out. But the man was so spiteful, so determined not to admit that Harry had been *right* all along, that he just wouldn't let it go and retreat to the cellar. Ben didn't deserve that gun, he didn't deserve to be in charge — Harry did!

Harry crept forward.

Helen saw it, knew what he was doing. She wanted to call out to Ben, to warn him, but there was so much noise and the door was still shaking and she knew that Harry *did* love Karen even if he didn't love her anymore and ... and so she froze.

Harry dove forward and snatched the rifle up from the floor. The gun was *his*!

Ben, still in full-pitched battle to keep the dead from breaking into the house, gaped at Cooper in dumbstruck awe. He had known that the man was an opportunistic asshole, had had the point driven home when he'd left Ben outside to die, but ... now, of all times? *Now*? Could anyone be *that* nearsighted, that *stupid*?!

Cooper, hunched over like a little troll, cocked the rifle as he backed away. "Go ahead! Go ahead!" the man blathered. "You wanna stay up here now?!" He pointed at his wife, then over his shoulder. "Helen, get in the cellar."

Ben tried to watch Cooper, but he couldn't dismiss the window. If he let go for one second, the dead might get in!

Helen also remained at her post, her back pressed to the barricade of the front door. She glanced at Ben, then looked back at Harry ... and shook her head.

"Get in the cellar now!" Cooper yelled at her. And whether he was conscious of it or not, he pointed the rifle right at his wife as he demanded, "*Move!*"

But it was Ben who moved.

Pulling the diagonal board from the window — it had been knocked completely loose by this point, anyway — Ben hurled the wooden plank at Cooper with all his might. The board struck the rifle across the barrel before flipping onto the sofa, knocking the gun down toward the floor (and saving Helen Cooper's life) as it discharged, the bullet slamming harmlessly into the rug.

Ben lunged at Cooper, knowing it was down to the wire — whatever might happen with the dead, he wouldn't live if Cooper held onto that gun.

They struggled, each with two hands on the rifle, each twisting it back and forth in an effort to shake the other loose. Cooper bared his teeth in a vicious snarl, the gleam in his eyes little better than those things outside.

Helen watched, watched her husband devolve before her. It was difficult to see in the gloomy house, but she could see enough to know that — no matter who won the fight — she would not be joining her husband in the cellar. She would carry her sick daughter up into the attic if she had to, but she would never lock herself in a room with Harry Cooper, would never turn her back on him ever again.

In the end, size, youth, and fitness won out, and Ben knocked Cooper to the floor with the butt of the rifle as he yanked it free. He turned the weapon around, cocking it and taking aim.

Cooper gazed wide-eyed up at Ben.

Helen, trembling, watched from the front door. Watched, and tried not to think about what she *wanted* to happen next, what she *wanted* Ben to do.

Ben hesitated for a moment as Cooper used the wall behind him to stand up, his hands open and pleading for mercy ... but only for a moment. Things had gone too far, the man had committed too many crimes to ignore. Beating him before had achieved nothing — if Ben let him live, it would only be a matter of time before he regretted it.

He would do what had to be done.

And so the civilized high school teacher tightened his grip on the rifle and shot the salesman.

The bullet hit Cooper in the left side of his gut — Cooper grasped at the wound, stumbled forward against the old piano near the cellar door, then slumped to the floor.

Ben stared down at the man as smoke drifted from the barrel of the gun. He knew he should feel something — regret at least, if not horror at what he had just done.

But he felt nothing. Nothing at all.

Then Helen screamed. Not over seeing her husband shot, but because the front door was actually beginning to splinter, the wood caving in under the pounding of rocks and fists and God knew what else.

Ben looked behind him and saw that the window he had left unattended was in danger of full collapse as well. He afforded Cooper one more glance, then turned away and rushed back to his own station.

The upper-left portion of the front door gave way, and Helen cried out as cold, dry hands reached through and grabbed at her right shoulder. She swatted at the hands, knocking them aside and pulling them away, but for every inch she gained, she lost two — they were pulling at her clothes, tangling into her hair!

Barbra watched from the sofa, then covered her eyes. It was so much like the man in the cemetery, pawing at her, biting at her, wheezing that horrid breath against her face — she couldn't stand it! She turned away from Helen ...

... and saw that Cooper was getting to his feet!

At first she thought that he had turned, that he was one of *them*! But instead of moving toward her, of reaching out and snapping his teeth at her, he shoved himself up along the piano and staggered *away* from the others, back into the open cellar doorway.

Harry Cooper was indeed still alive, but he knew he wouldn't be for much longer. The pain in his gut where the son of a bitch had shot — *shot* him! — was so intense, he couldn't give it proper expression ... and yet, at the same time, he found himself strangely numb all over.

All he could focus on, all he could think of, was to get to the one person who hadn't betrayed him this night — to get to Karen, his sweet baby girl.

Falling back through the cellar doorway, Harry forced himself to climb down the stairs. It was a clumsy affair, with none of his limbs knowing quite what to do anymore; his feet dragged over each step as his legs pumped forward, and it was nothing short of a miracle that he didn't tumble head-over-heels all the way to the bottom. By the time he reached the cellar floor, clinging to the wall for support, his vision was blurring and his breath was rasping in his throat. In the back of his mind, he noted that there was too much light down here, that with the power out it should have been like descending into a mine shaft ... but that would have meant that Ben was right, that some of the fuses had blown rather than the power lines going down as a whole, and even with his dying breaths, Harry Cooper didn't want to admit to being wrong, *especially* to Ben, so he dismissed it.

None of that mattered. The only thing that mattered was getting to Karen.

He ran a sweaty hand over his face, squeezed his eyes shut, then reopened them. When his vision refused to improve, he lurched onward anyway. He teetered from side to side, rocking wildly but somehow managing to stay on his feet. He made it almost all the way to his daughter's cot before collapsing onto his right knee, then forward onto his right hand, the wrist creaking in protest without his feeling it.

He reached out with his left hand, toward Karen, toward his little girl ...

... and then the concrete floor rushed up to meet him. He thought his fingertips brushed Karen's shirt as he fell, but his hands had grown so numb, he couldn't be sure.

Harry Cooper's final thoughts were, *I was right all along. It* is *dark as a tomb down here after all. I was right! I was right ...*

The world was growing dark for Helen Cooper as well. The more those things destroyed the barricades and broke through the windows and door, the more moonlight was leaking into the house, but all of that was overwhelmed by the dead hand that had found its way around her throat, cutting off her air. She clutched at it and tried to pull it away, but she could only catch the faintest snatches of breath — she was seconds from blacking out if Ben didn't come help her, but as her eyes rolled to the side, she saw that he was fighting his own losing battle; no aide would be coming from Ben, not in time.

In the end, it was Barbra who came to her rescue.

Still sitting on the sofa, her hands covering her face, Barbra was peeking through her fingers like a teenage girl at a horror film who, in spite of her fear, still wants to know what's coming next. And as she watched Helen's struggle, watched the door collapsing and falling away in pieces behind the woman, her eyes widened in disbelief.

Reaching through the widening gap at the top of the door was the man from the cemetery, the creature who — as far as Barbra was concerned — *started* this whole nightmare by attacking her and hurting Johnny!

For the first time in hours, Barbra came alive.

Snatching up the board Ben had used to knock aside the rifle in Cooper's hands, Barbra clenched her teeth and rushed across the room, centering her sights on the hand that was choking Helen to death. With her whole body weight behind it, Barbra slammed the board against the dead man's forearm so hard that, even over the growing noise, she heard one of the bones snap! The hand spasmed open, and Helen gasped a deep breath before falling away from the door.

Then all those hands flailed toward their new victim — Barbra.

She screamed as they grabbed at her, but not just from distress. Pent-up anger flowed from her, anger which had been percolating deep within her gut even as her mind had strove for denial and withdrawal. She cried out as the hands pulled at her hair, at her clothes, but she made no effort to pull away — she fought them, fought to keep the barricade intact, to keep the house safe.

She knew it was probably a lost cause, but the important part was that *she fought*!

Helen Cooper knew she should return the favor and help Barbra, but as soon as she realized that Harry was no longer where he had fallen, her heart clenched with a very different kind of panic — *Karen!*

Sailing down the basement stairs so fast her feet were a blur, Helen called out, "Karen?!"

She found the same patches of light as Harry, but she paid no mind to that mystery; nor did she give another thought to returning to help Ben and Barbra upstairs — in fact, in that moment, she forgot that Ben or Barbra existed.

For unlike Harry, Helen did not find her sick little girl passed out under her borrowed sheets. She found Karen up and about, kneeling before the body of her father ...

... and eating his arm.

"Karen?" she whispered.

Karen's eyes rolled toward her mother, and the hunk of meat from her father's shoulder fell to the floor. She moved around on her knees and, with some tottering, climbed to her feet.

"Karen ..." Helen said again, her voice taking on a pleading tone. She moved to the side, desperate to unsee what she was seeing.

Karen moved toward her, her arms outstretched as if seeking a hug. But the hunger in her young eyes and the gore covering her mouth told another story.

"Poor baby," Helen choked, tears filling her eyes ... but she still backed away.

Karen advanced, showing no emotion beyond that need, that monstrous *hunger*.

"Baby ..." she said again. Then her foot caught against something, and she stumbled and fell.

As soon as she hit the floor, striking her head on the corner of something wooden and unyielding, Helen's confusion sharpened into focus. What she was seeing was terrible, but she was no longer in denial of it.

As if to illustrate that point, Karen reached out and grabbed a dirty old trowel from the wall. Whatever had taken those things upstairs so long to figure out tools, Karen was apparently not experiencing the same delay — she grasped the little shovel's handle in both hands and raised it high above her head, ready to strike, as she again advanced upon her mother.

Helen wanted to get up, to run away, but her body was in revolt. Instead she cowered, unable even to form words to beg for mercy, for her daughter to stop this.

Helen was unable to speak, but she found she could still scream. She screamed as Karen stood over her and brought the trowel down, plunging the grimy metal into her chest. She screamed as Karen withdrew the tool and struck again, and again, and again, splattering Helen's blood across her face and onto the walls and all over Karen's dress which Helen had made for her last Easter. She screamed until she could scream no more ...

... and still Karen brought the trowel down again, and again, and again.

Upstairs, Ben and Barbra were not fairing a great deal better. The dead were swarming over the front of the house, threatening to crash their way in through sheer weight of numbers. To make matters worse, the gaps in the window were now sufficient enough that Ben was in serious danger of getting *bitten*, forcing him to fall back, literally, so that he could regroup and approach the window from a safer angle. At least the window started at waist-height — if Ben failed here, those uncoordinated things would still have some difficulty getting through it more than one at a time. But if they lost the barricade at the front door ...

Barbra was more than making up for her hours of useless catatonia. She fought like a woman possessed, keeping pressure against the barricade in spite of the octopus of arms that grabbed at her, and slapping and pounding at those grasping hands wherever she could. "No! No!" she cried over and over, but it did not come out lost or defenseless. She was terrified to be sure, but there was also wrath in her tone — Ben would not have been surprised if *she* had started biting at *them*.

But then the strength of her verbal denials began to slip. Against her best efforts, the loose door that Ben and Cooper had nailed across the entrance cracked and snapped as it was wrenched from its bonds. With one final "No!" from Barbra, it twisted free and fell, taking half of the smaller lumber with it. Once this barrier was gone, the front door itself gave up the ghost.

Then Barbra locked her gaze on one particular dead man and froze.

The first thing Barbra registered were those familiar driving gloves as a hand snaked in to close on the doorframe. Then she saw his face, still blood-streaked and now a sickly pallor. Her eyes bulged and she screamed so loud it overwhelmed everything else. *"NO! GET OUT!!!"*

Johnny did not listen. But then, he had never listened to his sister.

Barbra stared at him, praying, *pleading* for some spark of recognition. At any moment Johnny would remember her face, her voice, and go away. He wouldn't hurt her — he had died *protecting* her!

Johnny stretched out that gloved hand, reaching for her.

"No," she implored him. "No!" Then, when his

fingers clamped down on her collar just below her throat, she screamed, "*NO! JOHNNY, NO!*"

Ben saw it happening and, abandoning his own lost battle, rushed to help her.

"*No! No!*" Barbra cried as Johnny wrapped his arms around her. "*Help me!*" She beat at his shoulders, his neck, his face, all to no avail.

Ben reached for her, but her brother was already turning away, dragging her outside — for a moment, it stemmed the flow of the dead trying to get into the house, but that didn't protect Ben from all those grasping hands as he tried to get to Barbra, to save her. He couldn't fire the rifle, not at these close quarters, not without risking hitting her, so he used it as a club, tried to bash his way to her.

"Help me!" Barbra's voice was getting weaker, little more than sobs now. "Oh, help me. Help me ..."

And Johnny carried her into the arms of the waiting dead.

Ben tried and tried, and nearly died himself for his efforts. They were pawing at his face now — he had to retreat or risk having his eyes scratched out. Many of them were distracted by the feast Barbra's brother had brought out onto the porch, but there were plenty more to take their place.

Then the window gave way, and they were coming into the house through there as well.

Ben backed away, toward the cellar door — much as it burned to admit it, Cooper had been right all along. The house was lost.

He didn't see Karen stalking up behind him, and when she grabbed his arm, she missed sinking her teeth into his wrist by mere inches. He grappled with the little girl as she clawed at his face, her dead eyes glistening in the dim light, her teeth gnashing and her gory, fetid breath wafting up to repulse him.

He finally dropped the rifle against the piano long enough to pick her up and throw her away from him — she landed halfway onto the sofa and wasted no time getting back to her feet and coming at him again.

Ben seized the rifle and backed into the cellar entrance, slamming the door before the dead little girl could reach him. She collided with the door and shoved at it, trying to get through to him, to finish what she started. Ben leaned against it, shoving into place the crossbars Tom and Cooper had assembled as fast as he could.

The dead funneled into the house through the door and window — their prey was no longer in sight, yet they were driven by inertia, looking all around, searching every which way for the flesh they craved, the warm meat.

One particular dead man, whom Barbra would have identified as the man from the cemetery, spotted the little girl, saw her pushing against the cellar door. Somewhere in the chaos, he had ended up with the table leg, Ben's old torch, and as he knocked aside chairs crossing the room, he dragged it behind him. When he reached the cellar entrance, he heaved it over his shoulder and started slamming it against the door.

This drew the attention of many of the others, and soon the dead were bottlenecked at the cellar door, writhing and shoving and beating to get through. They were the embodiment of mob mentality: New dead men and women entered the house, saw the commotion, and joined in — some pounded the walls, or even each other, with their fists; others experimented with whatever tools were close at hand; one of them even started rocking the piano, slamming it against the wall.

The cellar door was quaking on its hinges as Ben slid crossbar after crossbar into place — hell, the entire wall was shaking! The door was as secure as he could possibly make it, and still it threatened to collapse.

Maybe *he* had been right all along, but not about staying in the cellar versus protecting the house. It was something he had said to Cooper, something flippant, when the little bulldog had described how those things would eventually show up by the hundreds — Ben had remarked, "Well, if there're *that* many, they'll probably get us *wherever* we are."

That certainly looked to be the case now.

There was nothing more he could do — the door, the *wall,* would either stand or it wouldn't. Holding a vigil at the top of the stairs would accomplish nothing, so he collected the rifle and climbed down the stairs.

Then he saw Harry Cooper, gazing with blank eyes up at the ceiling, his right arm a bloody stump. He wasn't sure how to feel about that — he had, after all, shot the man himself — but he *was* troubled when he turned his head away only to find Helen Cooper lying near the far wall, a trowel sticking up from her butchered chest.

He had hated Cooper, but he had liked Helen. And now, just like all the others, here they both were in the much-vaunted cellar, dead.

Dead.

That notion, and what it entailed, had only the briefest of moments to sink in for Ben ... and then Cooper was sitting up.

Ben stepped forward, cocked the rifle, took aim. Strangely, he found it *more* difficult to shoot the man now than when he had been alive upstairs. But in the end, that didn't change anything. It had to be done.

Ben shot Cooper in the face. And then, for good measure, he shot him twice more.

He turned away, leaning against a pillar and pressing

his forehead against his wrist. His adrenaline flow was slowing, and he found he was more exhausted than he had ever been in his whole life — his muscles quivered, his bones ached, his eyes stung ...

But he couldn't rest. Not yet.

Straightening, he stared at Helen Cooper, still lying where he had first seen her.

Maybe it would be different with her. She was lying with the back of her head against a box — maybe she had damaged something when she had fallen, maybe her brain was already too ...

Helen's eyes opened.

Ben cocked the rifle.

It had to be done.

So Ben shot the lovely woman in the head, shot her because she was dead and about to get up and eat him.

The tears which wracked his body were sudden and intense. Choking with sobs, Ben threw the rifle across the cellar, then assaulted the makeshift cot where Karen had died, knocking the blankets and door and sawhorses asunder. He stood in the middle of the room, covering his face, wishing it were over, wishing *he* were dead if that's what it took to escape this nightmare ...

And then, as always, his reason won out. Always and forever the pragmatist, Ben calmed down and considered his next step.

The dead had overrun the house. If they *did* break through the barricade, he would need another line of defense.

As much as he wanted to, Ben could not give up. That just wasn't the way he was made, that wasn't ... *Ben*.

He turned around in a slow circle, considering his options. He tried lifting the door he had knocked to the floor, then switched to one of the sawhorses. One was too cumbersome, the other too flimsy on its own; neither would prove useful without the hammer and nails, and both of those were somewhere upstairs.

In the end, Ben settled for recollecting the rifle and crouching down in the far corner of the cellar, the gun aimed at the bottom of the stairwell. He wiped sweat from his face and blinked away the urge to close his eyes, to sleep.

He would never give up, never. But there was nothing more he could do at the moment, not until the dead settled down, maybe forgot about him and wandered back out of the house. All he could do for now was wait.

Wait for the dawn.

In the house above, the dead pounded and ambled and explored. A few remained focused on the cellar door and adjoining wall, but most had forgotten about that. They spread through the house, some going from room to room, others drudging along in small circles. Different items caught different interests, from the furniture to the curtains to the fireplace — the bathroom mirror proved quite popular.

They had forgotten the flesh for the time being; the house itself was their fascination now. And it was theirs, here and across the country, as the faintest echoes of their former lives tugged at their failed minds. Here and everywhere. Homes, cars, shopping malls ... any of it, all of it.

Whatever struck them, flesh or fixtures, they wanted. And what they wanted, they took.

They were the living dead, and this was their night.

DAWN

Sunrise stretched over the land, chasing the night into retreat. Birds broke into song while crickets closed their shift. A very gentle breeze sighed through the fields, washing away the scent of death. Peace reigned, and anyone who had not personally lived through the night would have found it difficult to believe the things that had happened, that had risen.

Then the chirping of birds was joined by another sound, a manmade sound — a helicopter, running patrol over and ahead of the roving groups of armed men ... and just like that, the illusion of peace ended.

Rifles, pistols, guns aplenty. The squads pushed on, driven by duty for some, motivated by an unspoken glee for others. Order would soon be restored, of that they were confident, but for now, anarchy ruled.

Taking advantage of an open field, the helicopter circled around for a landing, and the patrol lines came together for a meeting-of-the-minds, so to speak. Police vehicles, including several K-9 units, joined the party, and those on foot took the opportunity to take a load off, to plop down on the grass for a welcome rest.

Chief McClelland strode through the ranks, wiping sweat from his brow with a handkerchief and heading toward his right-hand man, Vince, his deputized "lieutenant" for the day's festivities. McClelland called out to the man, who regarded him without rising to his feet; Vince just craned his head back to listen, chewing on a stalk of grass.

"We're gonna get about four or five men," the Chief told him, *"and a couple a dogs ta the house over here behind those trees, we wanna go check it out."*

Vince nodded and climbed to his feet.

McClelland then realized that the reporter, Cardille, and his cameraman had resurfaced and joined him — they sipped coffee from small white cups and looked far more rested than the Chief himself felt. "You still here, Bill?"

"Yeah, Chief," the reporter said, *"we're gonna stay with it 'til we meet up with the National Guard."*

McClelland nodded, but his eyes were on their hands. "Where'd you get the coffee?"

"One of the volunteers," Cardille answered, then pushed the cup forward. *"You're doing all the work, you take it."*

"Thank you," McClelland said, accepting the cup with sincere appreciation.

The reporter nodded, then replaced the caffeine with another vice — he took a drag from a cigarette.

"We should be wrapped up here 'bout three or four more hours," McClelland said. *"We'll probly get inta Willard then. I guess you can go over there an' meet the National Guard."* He leaned over and raised his voice, *"Nick, you an' the rest of these men wanna come with me?"*

Adjusting his rifle's shoulder strap, McClelland headed off, leaving the news crew alone.

"Well, Bill," the cameraman said, *"I'm gonna check with the office, see what's happening."*

"All right, Steve," Cardille replied, *"tell 'em we're going to stay with it and, uh ..."* He thought for a moment, then decided, *"... everything appears to be under control."*

As if to dispute his proclamation, some of the dogs

from McClelland's group started barking. But then, that had been happening all night. There were many dead wandering the area, and the dogs loathed their unnatural scent.

Cardille wasn't worried. After all, the dogs were with McClelland, and however unrefined the Police Chief came across at times, he had proven he knew what he was doing.

They were in good hands.

In the basement, Ben's head sunk lower, and lower ... until, for the one thousandth time, he stirred back to awareness. Partial awareness, anyway. His mind was so fuzzy, his thoughts so sluggish, there were times when he wasn't entirely sure that he *was* awake, considered that maybe he was only *dreaming* that he was awake, that the dead had broken through the barricade and were creeping up on him even now.

Funny, that *that* was what he should consider the dream at this point. No more delusions that the entire event was the nightmare, that he would wake up on the bus to discover a world where the dead had never risen ...

No, this was his reality now. All he could hope for was ... was ...

Was that barking?

Ben stirred for real now. He hadn't heard anything resembling *life* for hours now, and even before he had retreated into the cellar, there had been only crickets or other insects — no dogs, no cats, no livestock in spite of this being an old farmhouse. There had been just himself, Barbra, and the rest of the group.

So what did it mean that he could hear dogs barking?

The dogs' lead proved true. They zeroed in on some dead wandering the field behind the house the Chief had spotted earlier. A man and a woman ... or rather, a male and female — as far as the Chief was concerned, they weren't human enough to be called "man" or "woman," not anymore.

Two uniformed police officers drew their sidearms and started firing.

Gunshots! Those were gunshots!

Ben's hopes soared, but with some reservations. The sound of gunfire definitely meant there were people up there, but it did not guarantee that the cavalry had arrived. It could be other refugees like himself, who had seen the house and were seeking shelter, only to be taken by surprise as the dead burst outward to greet them.

His heart pounded. He wanted to believe that he had been rescued. But he had been through so much, *done* so much this night that his usual optimism was depleted almost to nothing.

What should he do?

A station wagon from the Willard Department of Public Heath rolled up the drive toward the group near the old farmhouse. As soon as they heard the shots, the driver and his partner had known it was back to work. Of course, these days their work was a hell of a lot more interesting than before this shit hit the fan.

They slowed down by Chief McClelland, who was standing near a burned out pickup truck. But he waved them on. "They need you down there by the barn," he told them.

"Okay," the driver acknowledged, then rolled on.

McClelland turned back to his group. "A couple of you guys just follow the wagon down, I wanna get a few men ta check out the house."

As they dispersed, McClelland returned his attention to the destroyed truck, and the stray human remains therein. He said to his lieutenant, "Somebody had a cookout here, Vince."

Vince agreed, "Yeah, sure looks like it, Conan."

Shaking their collective heads, the group moved on toward the house.

Ben was fully awake, or the closest he could come to it. A siren! Police car, ambulance, fire truck? It didn't really matter. A siren meant a vehicle, and that suggested a vast improvement on the situation out there in the real world.

And yet, still he held his spirits in check. He had to be smart about this, he had to be sure.

Slowly, one step at a time, Ben climbed the stairs toward the still-intact cellar door, straining his ears for every sound, every clue.

McClelland led his group onward, clearing out the dead as they went. Policemen, civilians — they all got their shots in. Though they would never admit it, some of them missed the head-shots on purpose, taking the opportunity to shoot the dead in the limbs or torso once or twice before finishing them off. Who could blame them? When would they again have the opportunity, the legal sanction, to shoot down actual people, dead or not?

After this, deer hunting would never be the same, that was for sure.

Ben reached the top of the stairs. Setting the rifle down, he eased the crossbars from the cellar door, trying to make as little noise as possible. He couldn't hear the dead in the house anymore, hadn't heard them for a while, but that didn't mean they weren't still out there, waiting for him.

Another dead male went down, clutching at its face as the bullet bore into the back of its head and exited through its nose. It was an almost-human reaction to the injury, but McClelland knew better — he had seen what these

*things did to real people, and knew not to attribute any
humanity to them at all.*

*The Chief rushed forward to confirm the kill, his
posse on his heels, then nodded in satisfaction. "He's a
dead one." He shouted to those who had fallen behind to
take care of a few dead stragglers. "Get up here!"*

The group converged.

*McClelland considered the number of dead they had
just put down, then shouted more orders. "Nick, Tony,
Steve ... you wanna get out in that field an' build me a
bonfire!"*

Ben opened the cellar door just an inch at first. Then,
when the dead did not pour over him like a flood from
Hell, he opened it further and peered out into the room
beyond.

The place was in a shambles, but there was not a dead
man or woman in sight.

Treading softly, he emerged from the cellar. The door
and walls were a mess, and the floor was littered with
flotsam from all over the house. The dead had moved a lot
of stuff around — sometimes to use as a tool to pound at
the cellar door, other times to ... to what? To study it?
Remember it?

But now the house was empty, with only the lingering
smell of decay to suggest the dead had ever been here.
Even the front door — what remained of it, anyway — had
swung back into a closed position.

Then Ben thought he heard muffled voices from the
front of the house.

Circling around to the window, he crept forward,
holding the rifle at ready without even realizing he was
doing it.

He wanted to see his saviors first, before announcing
himself. He wanted to be sure.

"You," McClelland ordered, then pointed at their latest kill, "drag that outta here and throw it on the fire."

Two men returned from checking the other side of the house. "Nothing down here."

"All right, go ahead down and give 'em a hand." He turned back to his lieutenant and said, "Let's go ahead and check out the house."

But Vince was already at attention, his focus on the broken front window. "There's something in there," he told the Chief. "I heard a noise."

His breathing shallow, his heart pounding, Ben edged toward the window, his finger on the trigger in case the dead should pop up like a sick Jack-in-the-Box. He could see people out there now, but his eyes were still adjusting from the darkness of the cellar. He just wanted to be *sure...*

Yes, yes! He could see them moving with a purpose. And he could hear them talking, something the dead never did.

They were real people. Living, breathing people.

He was saved.

Vince raised his rifle, lined up the sights.

"All right, Vince," McClelland encouraged him, "hit 'em in the head. Right between the eyes."

The thing in the house stepped far enough into the light for Vince to see it better, which helped his aim. That was great — he really wanted to impress the Chief, maybe turn this deputization into a permanent job when this was all over.

Bang!

The bullet struck the thing in the forehead and it went over backward.

Funny — for a second there, it had looked like the dead man was carrying his own rifle, but that couldn't be.

These things were too stupid to use guns. Unless ...

"Good shot!" McClelland declared, and Vince's pride swelled to eclipse any doubt that other rifle might have instilled, crushed any lessons that might have been learned that morning at the farmhouse.

"Okay, he's dead," McClelland continued, "let's go get 'im — that's another one for the fire!"

*   *   *

Perhaps it was a blessing in disguise that Ben was struck down that morning. Had he survived, had he called out and saved himself from Vince's bullet, he would have served witness to a world that would have turned his stomach.

Ben could not, of course, see how the hunters approached his corpse, not with respectful hands, but with meat hooks. He could not see the hooks driven savagely into his chest and abdomen, nor the way he was dragged from the house, down the porch steps and across the grass; the way they doused him with gasoline and tossed him onto a pile of wood, some of which was the very same lumber he had used to board up the house, to try to protect himself and those within; how the bonfire was lit, sending black, noxious smoke into the morning sky.

It wasn't the naked fact of these actions that would have disturbed Ben. Ever the pragmatist, he would have been among the first to argue that it needed to be done, would have shared his own experiences in the farmhouse as evidence of that belief.

No, what would have troubled Ben, would have left him feeling chilled and sickened, was the *carelessness* with which these actions were carried out, the callous and neglectful manner of his hurried cremation — treating it with the same dignity given to burning compost or old tires.

For while expedience was necessary, would it have harmed the men or their mission to have a moment of silence? For one or two of them to have said a small prayer, even just one or two words? And was that really, truly *delight* in their eyes when the next dead man or woman staggered over the ridge only to be riddled by bullets from every angle, or perhaps even captured and strung up for target practice?

The cold detachment the men embraced so readily, so willfully, would have shocked the school teacher, made him question whether the human race *deserved* what was happening to them, to reflect over the ultimate *reason* for the night of the living dead.

Ben had been skeptical of the so-called "radiation theory" before, and after witnessing this atrocious behavior, that skepticism would have evolved.

Maybe it wasn't radiation at all, he would have suggested, or a chemical weapon, or a germ or virus, or aliens from outer space, or any of the other popular theories.

Maybe, Ben would have suggested, there was simply no more room in Hell.

ABOUT THE AUTHOR

CHRISTOPHER ANDREWS lives in California with his wife, Yvonne Isaak-Andrews, and their Pug, PJ. He is working on his next novels, and continues to work as an actor and screenwriter. He and his wife are expecting their first child at the end of this year.

Excerpts from all of Christopher's novels can be found at www.ChristopherAndrews.com.

Breinigsville, PA USA
26 May 2010
238733BV00001B/40/P